Tracy Chambers knew there [illegible] victories in the ghetto. There were ju[illegible]ith a temporary absence of d[illegible]bold and beautiful novel[illegible]ess who surged up[illegible]to the heady[illegible]hion world.

The dazzli[illegible]ry of Tracy Chambers. Now a sensa[illegible]motion picture starring Diana Ross.

Mahogany

Burton Wohl

based on the original screenplay by
John Byrum
Story by Toni Ambler

CORGI BOOKS
A DIVISION OF TRANSWORLD PUBLISHERS LTD

MAHOGANY
A CORGI BOOK 0 552 10048 X

First publication in Great Britain

PRINTING HISTORY
Corgi edition published 1976

Corgi Books are published by
Transworld Publishers Ltd.,
Century House, 61-63 Uxbridge Road,
Ealing, London, W.5.
Made and printed in the United States of America
by Arcata Graphics,
Buffalo, New York

One

Pop-tops. That would do it. Tracy Chambers bent to her sketch block, smiling a secret and impudent smile. It was a fierce smile as well. She was serious. Seer-ree-uss! she hissed to herself under her breath, her slender shoulders hunched over the drawing table, her long, tapered fingers darting so quickly over the pebble-grained paper they were like swallows.

She paused and took a breath, her slim brown face concentrated and threatening—like an Egyptian queen. Her pen swirled and her brush dipped as she applied texture to the fabric of the daring little cocktail dress she was designing. Pop-tops, linked together like chain mail and falling just to the small of the back, worn like a gleaming cape over a silk-white sheath. Dazzling!

Use your own frame of reference, the instructor

had said. Be relevant. OK, Tracy thought; I can dig it. She'd been pelted with relevance ever since she was a teenybopper, ever since she'd raised her inch-long eyelashes and taken a clear, cold fix on the world around her. Relevance—it was a con word, like a whole lot of other con words that had come her way. It meant make do with what you've got, it meant settle for less. It meant keep on truckin'.

Well, this was relevance, all right. Pop-tops. Ripped off and discarded in the streets. Wasn't that what the South Side of Chicago was all about? She smiled to herself.

"All I asked you to do was sketch a simple little cocktail dress!" the voice came suddenly from over her head, and Tracy let six inches of daylight between her behind and the seat of her chair. She was back at ground zero now but her concentration was shattered.

"Something you can whip up at home. Something you can buy for twenty-nine ninety-five," the voice continued. "You're giving me grand opera."

Tracy laughed and looked around at the board-flat white woman who stared at her out of tired, ghetto-wise eyes. "You didn't say," Tracy said amiably, "where those cocktails were being had. I mean, this ain't no rag for a junior juicer. This is for your uptown mainliner. Like she's got so much bread she can get some little faggot to knit her up a cape made out of these pop-top gizmos for two hundred bucks—and never even drink the root beer!"

"Tracy—" her instructor began. And then she laughed and looked more carefully, admiringly at Tracy's sketch. "Will you listen to me," she said finally.

"Will you," she sighed, a sigh that stretched way back, over her own youth, her own frustration, her own vain fight to hack her way out of this ghetto, this urban wasteland, "will you remember that you've got to walk before you can run? Trust me. It'll save you time in the end."

"Sure I trust you, Margo," Tracy said easily, half meaning it, half shining her on, "only I got no time for walking."

"Right," Margo said and, knowing a lost cause when she saw one, she turned and bellowed to the class, "all right, people, pack up. Split city. Assignment's on the board, see you Wednesday night."

The bent heads rose, the quiet night-school class broke into noise and movement. Tracy looked around at a field of daisies, white daisies. She and another girl were the only black faces there. Was there a message in that? Oh, yes, she thought dimly, stuffing her belongings into an enormous tote bag and shrugging into her coat: the world of fashion was a white world, a very special garden shaded by money trees, fenced around with power. If you were aiming to get into that garden and if, along the way, you made the mistake of being black, you had about as much chance as a snowball in hell. Black snowball, white hell.

She sighed a sigh not unlike her instructor's, made her way out into the chilly night air and, when she was a safe distance away from her classmates, broke out a half-finished candy bar. Old habit, she grinned. When you grew up the way she did, you learned very quickly the first rule of survival: keep the goodies out of sight.

The wait for the subway was mercifully short and she broke out her sketch pad as soon as she gained her seat. It was an old habit, a way of keeping the squalor of the subway from denting her spirit. Ignoring the litter on the floor, the moronic advertisements and the graffiti sprayed from floor to ceiling, she settled into her fantasy world. It was her way of protecting herself from the aerosol agony, the rage, the longing, the sheer bewilderment which came out in dripping, badly spelled, and often obscene words. You had to turn your eyes away. To dwell on it was to feel the pain, the madness, all too close to your own.

As she finished a quick rough of a glamorous and frothy evening gown, she felt that the sketch was a little too empty, a little too pat. She looked up vacantly as the train slid into a station. A skinny black kid with knobby elbows and a spray can in hand was putting the finishing touches of what was clearly designed to be his masterpiece: FUCK THE BOARD OF MEDICLE EZAMINERS! he had written and he glared over his shoulder as the trainload of passengers disturbed his solitude. Tracy couldn't help grinning at him. He was so fierce, so awkward, so helpless, that she felt a surge of camaraderie. Astonished, the kid's eyes found hers and smiled back. He opened his mouth, perhaps to say something, but the train spurted air and began to move again.

Keeping her eyes on him for as long as she could, Tracy was delighted to see that the red streaks of his lettering were refracted by prisms of glass. Inspired, she began tugging at her colored pencils, filling in rainbow patterns on the gown she'd just designed.

A few minutes later, without looking up from her work, she automatically tucked away her pad and pencils, timing her movements so that she rose to her feet just as the car doors opened. As quickly and purposefully as a deer leaving the forest to cross an open meadow, all her senses alert to danger, she trotted down the ill-lit stairway to the street below. This cracked pavement—gum-spotted, beer-can-littered, trash-adorned—with its decaying storefronts, boarded-up windows, cruising police cars, drunks snoring in shadows—this was her turf. Two hundred yards to home. She clutched her keys in anticipation.

Soon Tracy became aware that something large and wine-smelling had picked up her track. She caught a reflection in a window glass. Drunk, but making good time. Staggering slightly but big enough, thickset enough so that he could be trouble. She could feel her scalp begin to sweat the way it always did when she was scared. And her own fear angered her. Shit! Why should she be scared. Why! And only a short distance from her home. She wasn't about to let this guy hit on her. Slowing slightly so that he could get closer, she suddenly turned and threw out one for him.

"Hey, baby," she said, waggling her tongue lasciviously, "you wanna buy yourself a piece of hard young ass?"

"Hunh? Whu? whu? whu?" the man stammered. There she stood, hip out, legs spraddled, eyes as cold as ball bearings. Offering it to him. Selling it to him. He could feel his lust collapse inside him like a thin plastic sack.

"Well how about it, sugar," Tracy said tartly, "I got business on my mind. You got the bread or ain't you? I'm sellin' pussy, man. You buyin'?"

The man shook his head. He was like an old bison who has just seen defeat. This girl, little bitty girl, so young, so tough. Frightening. There was no—no —he couldn't think of what it was, but something was wrong. He turned away muttering to himself, "Skinny little kid, little hooker, ain't no way, no way atall."

Then, making an obscene gesture so that he would remember her contempt for some time to come, she turned and resumed her lonely walk home. Victory? There were no victories in the ghetto, there was only a temporary absence of defeat.

Warily, quickly, both a little pleased and a little disgusted at her own stratagem—he was so easily crushed, so quickly routed—Tracy moved on. What had she wanted, she wondered. Defiance? Combat? Not quite that—spunk! That was it. Spark, pizzazz. But there wasn't much of that to be had in this neighborhood, she reminded herself. Underneath the swagger, the machismo, the violence, there was a layer of fear. And underneath that—nothing.

Turning the corner, she came to a quick halt. There, parked at the curb in front of her building, was a beat-up VW bus, lights on, engine running. And on top of the bus stood a wide-shouldered young dude in a leather jacket, talking through a bullhorn at some people leaning out of the upstairs windows. A bullhorn!

At eleven o'clock at night! Oh, shiiiiit! Tracy breathed. She was tired, her feet hurt, all she wanted was to get into bed and pull the covers over her head. Thrusting her hands deep into her pockets, she ground her teeth angrily. Just what she needed! A goddamn demonstration!

Hesitantly, wanting desperately to get into the safety of her apartment, yet dreading having to walk straight across center stage, she edged closer.

Brian Walker, the handsome young man on top of the bus, hadn't yet spotted her. Teeth flashing, shoulders dipping with an unconscious enemy, he half-danced through his pitch.

"Don't nobody throw us no quarters, hear!" he bellowed. "We ain't collectin' and we ain't the Good Humor man. This ain't the Good Humor truck. This the Bad Humor truck!" He laughed and the other sidewalk loungers and window-ledge watchers joined in. There was something about his voice, Tracy thought. It got to her, rubbed on her nerves like a fine emery board.

"You-all'd be in bad humor too," Brian Walker went on, "if it was *you* bein' thrown out in the street like Miz Johnson up there." He pointed dramatically.

"Hey, Lucille," a neighbor fat-voiced from another window, "you workin' up a lounge act wid this boy? You two gone play down at the Pic-a-Rib Sat'dy night 'n' Sunday?"

This brought a chorus of yoks.

But Walker wasn't going to let the fun get out of hand. Harshly, he shouted over the bullhorn, "This neighborhood's in deep shit! They goin' to pave right over you 'less you get outta the way. And when they got it all leveled down and paved over, they gone move you into them concentration camps. They call it a project! Project!" he said with contempt. "They won't stop kickin' out and tearin' down and pavin' over until this whole block's one big empty lot. Then, what you think they gonna do?" He paused dramatically.

A voice answered: "This damn block look a lot better if they did make it a vacant lot!"

"That's right, brother," Walker's voice was edged with sarcasm, "and you'd have one hell of a view of it –through the bars on your window. In the project. They put the damn bars up to keep people from pushin' each other out. That's the kinda hate builds up inside That's the kinda loneliness. You ever hear the suicide rate they got in them projects? Even the goddamn rats jump out the windows!"

This brought a chorus of assent, murmurs of agreement. Tracy, feeling trapped and impotent, like a child, decided to take two giant steps.

Brian Walker continued. "Now we're from the South Side Block Association. We gonna have people down here all day Wednesday. Over at the school. I'm puttin it to you: ten minutes of your time. That's all. Just ten minutes of your time to go over and sign the register. And it might just help save your house." He glared fiercely at the scattering of sidewalk loungers and curious householders. Was he getting through to them? Was the wall of apathy too high. Then he noticed Tracy nearing her doorway.

"At least there's one person," he said, his voice going silky, caressing. And Tracy felt it, damn him! Felt it where she didn't want to feel it. "There's one person here," Walker went on, "who is hip to home improvement. I mean we got a mighty fine improvement walkin' in here right now."

This got the laugh he'd intended.

"Scuse me, sister," Brian called out to Tracy–and she had no choice but to turn and look at him.

He smiled warmly. Goddamn it, he was handsome. She hated him.

"Sister, are you gonna take a few minutes on Wednesday to pick up on what you can do about keepin' your apartment in one piece? Keep it from gettin' bulldozed? Are you goin' to do that?"

"Oh, listen, brother," Tracy moaned, "I don't *got* any minutes. Not one. Not a couple."

"That's too bad," Brian Walker said, mockingly, "I guess you got important things to do. But tell me," he snapped, "what in the hell is more important than stoppin' some white landlord from throwin' you right out on your pretty little ass!"

"I'll tell you what I got to do, big brother," she said, loud and clear. "I got to work so I can make the bread to pay my rent with. You dig?"

"And even if you do pay your rent," Brian Walker was relentless, "what happens if you come home one day and you find a big hole where this building used to be?"

"I'll tell you the truth, mister," Tracy said, her temper getting the best of her, "I don't see that's any worse than coming home late at night to find some asshole blowin' at me through a bullhorn, so I can't get the sleep I need to do my damn job!"

Startled by the energy and concentrated anger of her voice, Brian Walker lowered the bullhorn from his lips and stared at her.

Tracy hesitated, some of the fight seeped out of her. His smile was devastating but his expression, when thoughtful, she found even more appealing. Damn him. "Listen," she stammered, "I'm–I'm just kinda tired–OK. I'm tired and I'm cold–and–"

"That's cool," Brian Walker said, "I can dig that. Once you get inside you can put your feet up and relax. But what about Miz Johnson up there? What's she gonna *do* out here in the street?"

"I don't know," Tracy mumbled helplessly. She was embarrassed now. She'd done the one thing she shouldn't have done, drawn attention to herself. She'd dug her own trap and now had barely the energy to get herself out of it.

"Oh, you don't *know!*" Walker said. He had her on the run now and his audience was with him. "You don't know? Or you don't care? It's *her* problem, is that right, little mama? Miz Johnson's problem, right? You just goin' on in and get yourself some sleep, is that it? Now I know what *you* goin' to do, but the question still is, what is Miz Johnson goin' to do!"

"I said I don't know," Tracy said wearily, but then a little quiver of energy overtook her, "but whatever she does it'd be a damn sight smarter than ridin' around on top of that bus and wagglin' that damn bullhorn like you was some kinda high-school cheerleader!"

"Hey, right on!" There was a chorus of laughter. Tracy, feeling she'd restored her dignity, turned to walk up the steps into her building. Unfortunately, at that moment a fat man in an upstairs window ripped the top of his beer can, causing a gush of foam to cascade to the sidewalk below. Tracy wore a cockeyed crown and a broad bib of suds.

Now it was Brian Walker's turn to laugh and he made the most of it. The crowd joined in. They were beginning to enjoy this. It was like a Punch and Judy show.

Tracy fumed. Close to tears, she attempted to wipe the mess from her face and front.

"Lean to the left!" Walker called out in singsong cheerleader fashion. "Lean to the right! Keep on truckin'—the towel's in sight!"

This brought a cheer but Tracy didn't hear it. She pounded into the doorway and raced up the stairs. Inside her apartment she switched on the lights, took one look at her dress, and collapsed in a chair. She was too far gone in anger, fatigue, depression, to do anything but sprawl.

As a general rule, her spirits rose when she entered her apartment. With brightly painted wicker chairs, posters, throw cushions, sketches, hanging plants, Japanese kits, and swatches of material, she'd turned her two-room home into something bright and giddy, gay and affirmative. It had life, spirit, hope—pizzazz.

And there she sat, in the middle of all that splashy color, all that bold invention, and all she could feel was the itch of self-pity tickling the back of her nose. "I'm not gonna cry!" she said aloud fiercely. And then to herself she whispered: Not! Gonna cry! Not! In another few moments the sensation left her. She peeled off her ruined, sodden dress and her beer-soaked underpants as well. Naked, sinuous, as lithe as a maiden eel, she slipped into her bed and fell sound asleep.

Next morning, after a quick breakfast of wheat germ and grapefruit juice, Tracy clipped briskly through the teeming streets of Chicago's garment district. Everywhere about her there was bustle and hustle, huge trucks double-parked, disgorging cartons and bales, bolts of cloth, taxicabs blasting their horns while beefy cops urged beefy truck drivers to move their vehicles before traffic congealed in a solid mass. Traffic on the sidewalks was no less dense. Swivel-hipped young blacks with crocheted headgear artfully pushed wheeled clothes racks between passersby, sidewalk hucksters, and knots of gossiping clothing workers. There was noise, dirt, color, movement, and over it all, the sweet high-spirited fragrance of new fabric. Pausing to ponder a window full of coat buttons spilled in bright profusion like stones from the sea, Tracy bent over slightly, only to snap straight like a switchblade when she was unmistakably goosed. Turning, she narrowly escaped stepping on a myopic old Jewish tailor with a cane, being bumped by a teenager whose arms were full of boxes, being run over by a maniacal clothes rack pusher. It could have been any or all of them, deliberate or accidental, and she dismissed the incident with a laugh.

Turning into the side door of a garment manufacturing firm, she managed to slide into the freight elevator just before the heavy iron door could pin her in a murderous embrace. Upstairs she stepped into a large loft already warm with the pale morning sun filtering through skylights. The smell was breathtaking —cheap perfume, sweat, machine oil, fabric, soggy coffee containers, and stale lunch boxes. The room was almost two acres in area and utterly packed with high-speed sewing machines operated almost entirely by women, more than half of whom were black.

Standing on her toes and craning, Tracy made out the form of her Aunt Florence, a frowning, hefty no-nonsense black lady, and she made her way through the aisles. Florence sat with her nose an inch or two from the dancing needle, thick fingers adroitly sliding the seams through the machine, her heavy arms shining with exertion. Thick knife welts on Florence's throat and upper arms testified to the fact that this woman was a survivor. Tracy adored her. She stooped impulsively and kissed the back of her aunt's neck.

"Jesus Christ!" Florence yipped and then, seeing her niece, grinned. "God love us, child! You almost made me sew that zipper on my thumb."

Tracy smiled and fingered the garment Florence had been sewing. "Any woman dumb enough to buy that kind of junk and at those prices, doesn't matter where you put the zipper. They wouldn't know the difference. Doesn't it make you sick to turn out this trash?"

"Honey," Florence said, "I musta tole you a hundred times–"

"I know," Tracy said, "this trash is my bread and butter. Still, Aunt Florence, with your talent and with your knowledge–my God!" Tracy stopped, awed by the possibilities she envisioned for this queen of the needle trades.

"Aw right," Florence said with a broad grin, "you gave me the treatment. I'm conned, OK? So what are you doin' here and why'd you bring that portfolio? As if I didn't know."

"Oh, I just happened to be dropping by and thought–"

"Yeah, you thought," Florence said, taking the portfolio from Tracy's hands and opening it. She quickly sifted through the sketches.

"Mm, mmm!" she said enthusiastically, "Tracy, girl,

you're gettin' good. Fact, too good for me. I'm just a backcountry girl, I never did learn how to make all that fancy stuff you got in there."

"Aw, come on, Aunt Florence, you could whip this up in no time. There isn't a French coutourier who knows as much about building a dress as you do."

"Well, young lady, I ain't one of them French–I hope that was a polite word you just called me–and another thing," she motioned to a plastic basket full of garments at her feet, "I'm up to my ass in work. I get two dollars and eighteen cents a piece on these mothers and the rent is due this week, you hear?"

"Hey, Florence," a fat white man called out around the stub of a soggy cigar, "you servin' tea over there at your machine? I want mine in a glass."

"Well, up yours, Baby Melvin," Florence called out cheerfully, "shove the glass–" And to Tracy she added, "That's Baby Melvin we call him, the boss's son. I better get back to work." Noticing Tracy's pout, she said, "OK, OK, gimme a couple days to work these things up. And Tracy?"

"Yes, ma'am?"

"They're good, child. I mean really good."

Tracy giggled with pleasure, threw a kiss to her aunt, and beat her way out of the loft. Unwilling to be assaulted by that freight elevator door, she trotted down the stairwell, her spirit so carbonated by her aunt's compliment that she didn't even notice the astonishing display of male genitalia spray-painted on the walls. Florence's fellow seamstresses were very proud of their collection; they had the best porno artists in the entire garment district.

As she turned into State Street and approached the main entrance of Marshall Field, Tracy felt the city and herself become more sedate, more temperate, even ostensibly sane. She strode briskly, through the revolving doors, scarcely looking at the lavish displays of luxury goods, picking her way expertly through the strolling shoppers so that she could get to the escalator in the fastest time.

Upstairs, she debouched into the handsome, sophisticated "28 Shop" and was overcome with something like a cathedral hush. Thick carpets underfoot, the smell of perfume in the air, soft music, and a general reverential hush made this a sort of church. The First Church of Heavy Schlock, Tracy muttered to herself, noting with some disdain the high-priced and ill-made merchandise which American women were accustomed to regarding as "boutique fashion." A tall and rather imposing white woman in her early forties detached herself from a group of window trimmers and display artists when she saw Tracy enter. Vectoring quickly so that she would intercept the girl she said tersely, "Tracy, bring your pad."

Without missing a beat, Tracy docily fell into step behind Linda Evans. Her work day at Marshall Field had begun.

As they traveled down the escalator to the main floor, the same route Tracy had just made, Linda Evans began a monologue which was different only in particulars from the one she'd been delivering to Tracy on and off for the past few months.

"I don't know," she said, "how they felt about your being late when you were a salesgirl, Tracy, but as a secretary, we have different expectations. I expect *my* secretary to be on time. *I* am on time and I want the people who work for me to be on time. Otherwise there is no reason for me to employ them. Do you follow? Now we have a great deal of preparation ahead of us. I don't have to remind you that Christmas is on the way. I don't have to point out to you what Christmas means to a great merchandise institution. In addition to that, we are expecting the great Mr. Sean McAvoy to photograph our collection—"

Tracy, as usual, having waited for the first salvo, broke in with her apologies. "I am so sorry, Miss Evans. I had a late class last night and on the way home, I was further delayed—"

"I thought we agreed, Tracy," Linda Evans said

tartly, "that if these night-school courses were beginning to affect your daytime performance, you'd give them up."

"But I do that on my own time, Miss Evans."

"I'm concerned with what you do on *my* time. There are six thousand employees in this store, Tracy. Most of them stand behind counters all day until their ankles puff up. I suggest you let your promotion to the display department satisfy you for the time being. If you have creative urges, satisfy them in some other way. It's better than having your ankles puff up. Do you follow me?"

"Yes, ma'am," Tracy said and added under her breath, You cunt! It shocked her. Had she ever called anybody that before? One of these days, she thought, one of these days. But there was no time for more thought. Linda Evans had paused in front of a new Christmas display being carpentered into existence and was rapping out orders with the speed of light. It was up to Tracy to record every one of these deathless commands on her steno pad. Oh, yes, she thought, addressing that great Job Interviewer in the Sky: I take shorthand!

Somehow the morning passed. Now and then, criss-crossing the huge floor area of the "28 Shop," Tracy paused to examine a new garment on a rack or draped in deceptively artless fashion over the back of a chair. Something would catch her eye, some fragment of excellence, some ghost of fine workmanship or first-class design. But these were echoes, tokens only. The garment itself was, in the inevitably Yiddish diction of the trade—high-class schlock or, even worse than this fakery, costly dreck. Garbage. Why did it happen, Tracy wondered. When would these manufacturers, jobbers, buyers ever learn? You *could* sell quality. She was convinced of that. There was a hunger for fine design.

Why did all these people labor so mightily, fighting, scrambling, competing, stealing the best designs of Paris, Rome, London, Dublin, and—yes, New York, and once having grasped these treasures, proceed to destroy them, cheapen them with subtle changes, reductions, substitutions.

She could understand the purely economic logic. After all, you could hardly expect a young American working woman to shell out eight hundred dollars for a Paris pantsuit. You had to substitute machine work for all that costly hand-sewn detail. But still! Still—the machines were so good, so clever. They could duplicate human fingers so closely that not even an expert could tell one from the other. Then why the great difference in workmanship?

It wasn't just a matter of economics, Tracy knew. It was something worse, more vicious. It was the unconscious response of small minds to the threat of talent. They were frightened by it, awed by it, aware they had no power before it, couldn't dominate and control it. So they did the one thing they could do: they destroyed it. They nibbled away at it like nervous rats. A button here, a placket there, a bit of braid removed, a rhinestone added. Voilà! a total adaptation to ticky-tack. Nothing to fear now, nothing to be in awe of. Good old American industry could run this through the hopper and let the buyer be damned!

All of this Tracy knew. And still she aspired. Burned. She was capable of good design—great design! And she would prevail, she would get her creations before the public. The well-heeled public, to be sure. She had no illusions about who bought good design and how much they were willing, indeed eager, to pay for it. What happened after that was not, could not be her concern. She knew she couldn't revolutionize the entire garment industry. Couldn't change the mentality of manufacturers and sellers all over the country. All she could do was her own thing. And she didn't doubt for a moment that she would.

At lunchtime she eased her way out of a crowded coffee shop carrying a sandwich and a container of coffee, content to eat her lunch as she strolled along the sidewalk. It was better than being elbowed, ogled, and–yes, goosed once more. She decided she'd have to reserve this silk jersey for times when she wasn't mingling with crowds, since it clung to her small but sharply defined little ass like the skin of ripe fruit. Suddenly, between bites and ruminations, she heard a familiar sound. It came out of a bullhorn and had a metallic and gritty overtone, but underneath it lay velvet.

Staring across the street, she located the beat-up VW bus and sure enough, there was Brian Walker, teeth flashing in his handsome face, haranguing a crowd of lunchtime idlers. She leaned against a lampost to watch.

"I know," he said amiably, "that a lot of you will be catching the train back to Winnetka at five o'clock." He had dropped his ol'-country-boy diction. He sounded urbane now, almost white. Intrigued, she continued to listen.

"To a lot of you," Brian went on, "Chicago is just one big shopping center. A place where you come to get what you need–and what you don't need. But a lot of other people *live* in this city. They live in little houses, shabby apartments that have made it through Illinois tornadoes, Lake Michigan winters, and some of 'em even got through the Chicago Fire. These houses have made this city what it is–and nothing is being done about them. Every available nickel for urban renewal is spent on keeping the Loop pretty. But what good is this Loop gonna do you if the whole city dies around it. I want you to think about that when you take the train back to Winnetka!"

Right on! Tracy thought, cheering him under her breath. And then, in the next moment, she felt a flush of irritation. Why did he bother? What was he getting out of this? What was in it for him, she asked with ghetto logic. Because it wasn't as if this was going to do any good. She didn't have to be a student of politics to know that. Taking one person out of ten on the sidewalk who paid any attention to Brian's pitch, fewer than one out of ten of *those* would do anything about it. So it was a gesture. A brave gesture perhaps. Most likely it was a scam, she reminded herself. Somewhere, somehow, he was on the take.

Brushing crumbs from her hands, she dropped her unfinished sandwich in a trash can and drained the dregs of cardboard-tasting coffee. Funny, she thought, he'd set up a little thrill of expectation inside her, something in his voice, his energy, some little flutter of hope. But just as quickly, it faded. There was only one thing to do about the problems of this city, this ghetto–leave it. Leave it far behind. She surreptitiously hiked up the waistband of her panty hose and walked briskly back to work.

Two

A few nights later there was a confrontation in Tracy's neighborhood. A wrecking crew, most of them white, a few black, had spent much of the day demolishing an old tenement. They were tired now, beer-bound and waiting for the foreman to pick them up in his truck. It wasn't the foreman who arrived, however. It was Brian Walker, boy agitator, who leaped out of his VW bus and directed his bullhorn at these weary hard hats who were in no mood for a sermon. While Brian was warming up to his spiel, Brian's good buddy and political lieutenant, Wil, hung out a hand-lettered sign which read, "Projects Turn People into OBJECTS!"

"The slumlords," Brian shouted, "jack up the rents so high nobody can afford to pay. Then they get the buildings condemned because nobody lives there. *Then–*" he paused for emphasis, "they turn around the next day and sell the land to the city. For a bundle! To put up projects. And I'm talkin' to you because they're doin' it to you! Not black. Not white. All of us!"

Brian paused again to gulp air and the heckling began. "Hey, buddy," one of the hardhats called out, "you're lucky we're fumigatin' this rathole for you."

Brian glared and muttered under his breath. Wil grabbed his arm. "Cool it, man," he murmured. "This is how you always blow it, remember?" Don't let 'em get to you."

Brian nodded, arranged his features in an ingratiating smile and cocked a finger at the hard hat as if to say: That's a point for you. The hard hat, expecting a counterblow, opened his eyes in astonishment and gaped.

Brian went on.

"There's a program in this city being neglected by the very people it was created for. People like you and me. These houses—these very houses can be bought for one dollar! Did you know that? Did you hear about that? No, you didn't. Because ain't nobody's telling you. One dollar!"

He paused to let this information sink in.

And it was during this pause that Tracy caught sight of the tableau. She was on her way home from work, her arms freighted with groceries. But when she saw Brian and his bullhorn, she stopped short. It was beginning to appear as if she were destined to keep falling over this dauntless young man. Once again she edged up to the gathering crowd.

Just as she did so, a construction truck came out of the demolition site and found its exit blocked by Brian's VW bus. The driver bellowed out of his window.

"Hey, move that goddamn thing before I run right over it!"

Brian hesitated, then put down his bullhorn and leaped into the van. Angrily slamming it in gear, he backed it up a dozen feet to clear the truck.

While he was doing this, Tracy had a mischievous impulse. Quickly pouncing on the bullhorn, she ripped a carton of milk and poured a pint or so into the open bullhorn. Then she set it carefully down on the bell.

A moment later, Brian swung out of his van, nimbly picked up his bullhorn, and was about to break into his pitch when a torrent of milk splashed all over his face and chest. His gargle and squawk were ludicrously amplified. The roar of laughter was instantaneous and the hard hats fell on each other like men who had never seen anything so funny in their lives.

That was all Brian needed. Singling out his most recent heckler, he launched himself at him head first like a reckless saloon fighter, and then the battle was on. Wil joined in and one or two other blacks who were supporting Brian entered the melee.

At one point in the scuffle Brian broke clear and thought he saw Tracy waving the milk carton at him and grinning like a little fool. For an instant he wondered if he'd just been had. But the instant didn't last long because the sirens began to bloom all around them and seconds later he was being hustled into a squad car.

Tracy, watching this swift police action, couldn't help noticing that only the blacks were taken into custody. Suddenly her practical joke tasted rancid on her tongue.

Later, when she had put her groceries away and was spooning up a cup of soup, she quizzed herself and came up with no satisfactory answers. It was a hostile act, sure, she knew that. But why? No answer. What had he done to her? No answer. Why had she let him get under her skin like that? No answer. Or, it might be more correct to say, no answer that she was willing to put into words.

Deep down inside she knew the answer all right. It was that Brian stood for something positive, affirmative, courageous, and even selfless. He appeared to be trying to do something for his people, something for his community. And all Tracy wanted to do was leave it. Abandon ship.

The realization shamed her. Not enough to make her alter her plans or her aspirations but enough to cause a gnawing sense of guilt. She knew she had taken it out on Brian. She'd have to make it up to him somehow. The very least she would do was to go down to the police station and try to get him sprung.

Next morning Brian, grateful though confused, shambled out of the precinct house after his night in jail. He hadn't slept very well and his clothes smelled of disinfectant but he had a bail-bond receipt in his hand and that was all that mattered. Smoothing his hair and tugging down his jacket, he was about to walk down the street when Tracy stepped away from the wall. Brian stopped short. He recognized her at once. You didn't forget a chick who looked like that. And then another thought came to him.

He squinted at the bail-bond receipt in his hand. "You wouldn't, by any chance," he said, "be—er—Tracy Chambers?"

"Guilty, your honor," Tracy said. And she turned the receipt over and read the name on the other side. "And you have to be Brian Walker, right? And, uh, if you want to get sore and do something about it, remember, we're only two steps from a police department."

"Just a minute," Brian said cautiously, "are you with Legal Aid, ACLU, NAACP—what *are* you?"

"I guess you might say," Tracy mumbled, "I'm sorter with the milk fund!"

"Oh, no!" Brian moaned. "You—with the—" he made a pouring gesture.

"Yeah."

"Why, for God's sake!"

"I don't know," Tracy said, "it just kinda came over me."

"Maybe you wanted to meet me real bad."

Tracy considered that. "It's a possibility, but I don't think so."

"Then why in the hell did you bail me out?"

"Well I did and I didn't," Tracy said cautiously.

"Baby, you better explain that. I'm pretty hot as it is, spending the night in the slammer all on account of something just kinda came over you."

"Thing is," Tracy said, "that check I gave the cops for your bail, a hundred dollars?"

"Yeah."

"Well, if you can't cover it, we're both in trouble. Me 'cause I gave them a bum check and you because it's your bail," she said.

Brian's face creased with pain. "You wrote a bum check and handed it to the Police Department!"

"Well," she shrugged, "I wasn't budgeting to have to spring anybody this month."

He grabbed her roughly by the shoulder and shoved her a few paces down the sidewalk. "Hey," she protested, "where we going?"

"You're going home and I'm going to have to scrape up a hundred bucks from somewhere," Brian said.

"Home! I can't go home," Tracy said, "I've got to get to work. I might've lost my job already."

Brian paused and looked at her. "Hey," he said, his voice softening with appreciation, "you really did go out on a limb for me, didn't you."

Tracy found herself flushing under his smile. There was that damn emery board feeling again. Damn him! Damn something.

"I just felt guilty, that's all," she snapped, "for making such an ass out of myself last night." And for right now too, her mind filled in.

"That's all there was to it," Brian smiled assuredly.

"Sure, what else?" Tracy defied him.

"Well, I'll tell you what we're going to do," Brian said suavely. "I'll just drop by your place with the money tonight so you can cover that check, all right? And then maybe we can come up with something for us both to feel guilty about. Together."

"I–uh–" Damn it! Tracy thought. Goddamn it! Why was she fluttering. Why was she falling all over herself like a little jerk. "Listen, Jack," she said sharply, "I don't think you got the signals straight. I just wanted–"

"Tonight you'll feel different," Brian said confidently.

"Tonight I'm gonna make up the sleep I didn't get last night when your little political rally was going on."

Brian's sure smile faded. He became conciliatory. "Lady, I just want to bring you the cash I owe you and tell you how much I appreciate your efforts–"

"Yeah, well you could carry it on your back in nickels and I still wouldn't let you in the front door." She began walking away. Why? Why had she fought him so hard? Why was she coming on quite so tough?

"Hey, wait," Brian called, "the money–"

"Stick it–" she said, and then took a deep breath, "in the mailbox."

He stood there, a puzzled smile on his face, watching her walk away.

As Tracy rushed past the windows of Marshall Field, something inside caused her to come to a halt. One of the display windows was full of movement and it was something other than the usual window dressers at work. A model, live, not a mannequin, had struck a languorous pose. Near her, a slender, grizzled photographer, wearing a battered army fatigue jacket, was snapping out orders and clicking away with his Nikon. He seemed to be in perpetual motion, click, snap, move, circling around the model, taking pictures as fast as the camera would function, and when it was empty reaching out to his assistant, without ever looking at him, for another loaded camera. Tracy was fascinated by this silent but electric scene on the other side of the windows. So fascinated, in fact, that she did not realize for some seconds that Linda Evans, her boss, was motioning to her angrily.

Inside the store, she made her way to the rear of the display window where the picture session was in progress. Now she could hear the photographer's voice, rhythmic, sardonic, commanding. "Pensive, meaning thoughtful, dummy, that's right. More. Brood. Turn. Too far. Left. Right. Extend the leg. Further. Let me feel it. Don't worry, I won't get you pregnant. Sore? Good. Don't sulk. Glare. That's it. Raise the head. Higher. Not too high. You've got gorgeous nose holes, darling. Three of them, but gorgeous. Look, be sad, will you. Sad, not bushed. You look bushed. Sad. Oh, shit! Take a break, will you, honey."

He turned wearily and was about to hand the camera back to his young assistant when his eyes fell upon Tracy, who in her eagerness had pushed into the doorway.

"Well, that's more like it," he said, snapping her picture as she gaped at him. "OK, darling, get your coat off. I'll do a few polaroids for the feel of you before we get you into wardrobe."

He turned to Linda Evans, "OK, now we're getting down to business, Evans. You get me six more dummies like this one and we can get this job done right."

"Six more–" Linda Evans gasped. "That's my assistant you're talking about, Mr. McAvoy. She isn't a model."

"The hell you say, honey."

"My assistant secretary, Tracy Chambers. This is Sean McAvoy," Linda introduced them.

"You're Sean McAvoy!" Tracy gasped with genuine delight. "Oh, I don't know what to say. I think you're the greatest–" She stopped, embarrassed at sounding like such a gushing little groupie.

He smiled and was about to speak, but Linda Evans broke in. "Tracy," she said imperiously, "do something about getting some chairs for those girls. And get some coffee for Mr. McAvoy and me. How do you take it, Mr. McAvoy?"

Shaking his head in frustration, McAvoy held up a hand to signify that he wanted no coffee. "Giulio," he rasped at his young assistant, "get a bottle of vodka out of my case and *faí presto*, OK?"

It became a long and exciting day for Tracy. She had to run her feet off on one errand after another.

But she also got to see the world's highest-paid and most highly honored fashion photographer at work and she thought of it all as a learning experience. Later on, however, sitting in her apartment in her bathrobe and rubbing her aching toes, she felt more than a pang of loneliness. It was Saturday night after all, and here she was, ground down to a nubbin, sitting alone in her apartment and nursing her sore feet. Her thoughts went back to the morning and she recalled Brian Walker's face, puffy with lack of sleep when he came out of the police station, and then quickly alert when he recognized her. He was too handsome for his own good, she thought. And too full of himself. He had ego smoke coming out of his ears. Hell, yes, he was attractive, but the kind of man who would come on strong and then forget about you a week later.

Something shuffled on her staircase outside the door and she looked anxiously to see that all her various locks and chains were in place. Some Saturday night drunk on the prowl, no doubt, and the best way to avoid trouble was to lock it out.

Then there was a knock at her door. She started. Should she answer it? Yes, the locks were in place.

She tiptoed to the door and listened for a moment. She could hear heavy breathing, but somehow it didn't sound like drunk breathing. "Who's there?" she asked tentatively.

"Brian Walker. Got to show you something."

"I thought I told you to put it in the mailbox."

"Yeah, well I can't, honey, that's what I got to show you."

Tracy hesitated. Then she unfastened the locks and opened the door just the amount permitted by a stout chain. "What is it you want to show me—"

Then she shrieked in surprise. A shower of brand-new gleaming nickles began to pour in through the crack in the door, piling up over her bare toes and running all over the floor.

"Stop it!" she shrieked, breaking into gales of laughter. But the torrent of nickels kept on. "Brian, cut it out, will you–all right, all right!" She pulled the chain back and he entered her apartment, carrying a half-empty money sack in one hand and a bouquet of tawny chrysanthemums in the other.

"Now," he said, "you gonna throw me out? If you do, you're gonna have to pick up all those nickels by yourself. Two thousand of 'em!"

"I give up," she said. "Come on, give me a hand with all of this. Wait, I'll get a broom and a dustpan."

"I got a better idea," he said. "You go change into something you wouldn't mind eating dinner in and I'll sweep up all this loot here. Know what?" he said. "I know a place where we can eat pretty good on a hundred dollars worth of nickels."

Hours later they emerged from a cozy French restaurant where they'd sat and talked easily as if they'd known each other for years. Tracy was astonished at his sincerity and his openness. He listened to her as though he were really interested in all she had to say, and reacted warmly, as if he really cared. Her natural caution made her a little skeptical, but her feelings inclined her to trust him. She felt certain he wasn't making a pitch. He hadn't tried to "come on" to her and it didn't seem as if he was on a giant ego trip either. She had been awfully wrong about Brian Walker, it seemed.

When he dropped her off at her doorstep, there was no takeover, no bear hug, not even a good-night kiss. "Tomorrow, if you're not doing anything, maybe we could take ourselves a little walk," he said to Tracy.

"Uh, sure, I'd love to," she said.

"OK, pick you up about twelve, that OK? Too early, too late?"

"No, I've got a little work to do but I'll have it done by then. Twelve would be fine. Sure you wouldn't like a cup of coffee," Tracy found herself saying and at the same time asking herself if she was losing her mind. Invite a virtual stranger in at one in the morning! What was she trying to prove?

"Thanks," Brian said, "this has been a lot of fun for

me, but I've got a hunch we could both catch up on some sleep. So I'll say good night to you, Tracy."

"Good night, Brian. And thank you."

He made a gesture and was gone.

Thank you, Tracy told herself, as she put all the locks in place, for not making a pass at me, for not trying to bullshit me and for not—she added wistfully—giving me a good-night kiss. Bastard, she thought. And went to bed.

The next morning Tracy, looking very much the *Vogue* model in a little number that she had designed and executed herself—with the help of Aunt Florence—found herself eating a hot dog with one hand and playing a fast game of air hockey with the other. It was a neighborhood bar and grill and Brian Walker was obviously well known. As Tracy concentrated on her next shot she heard a man walk up to Brian and murmur, "Hope you make it, my man."

Brian said nothing but there was enough in his silence so that Tracy knew the remark had nothing to do with air hockey.

"You know," Tracy said, as she straightened up, "there's something about you that you aren't telling me." She waved a hand to include this bar, the whole ambience.

"Well." Brian smiled. "The impression I got when we first um, er met was, you didn't have much of an appetite for politics, right?"

"That was the other night," Tracy said. "Anyway I'm not talking about politics, I'm talking about you. There's got to be more to you than just politics!"

"Unh, unh," Brian said easily, and managing at the same time to score a goal. "Politics is all there is—ever since I left the law firm."

"Law firm!"

"That's right. 'My son, the lawyer.' Made my mama and daddy very proud of me. I guess I was proud too for a while. Stood to make a lot of bread." He shrugged as if that were all past.

"OK," Tracy said, "now we're getting down to it. I mean, how do you live, Brian? That is, what do you do for a living?"

"Just what you've been seeing me do. What you're seeing me do right here in my turf, my precinct."

"You mean you went through law school, passed the bar, had a position with a firm–and gave it all up for this!" Tracy was incredulous.

Brian slammed a last shot into the goal. "That's it," he said, "game's over. Home team four, visitors–not so hot. Here," he said abruptly, "come on outside with me."

She took his hand and followed him out into the quiet Sunday street. Pale sunshine filtered through the smog and there was an air of–not quite serenity, rather, a sort of truce. "Let's walk," he said, "and maybe I can make it clear to you."

Without saying much more, they began to walk the cracked and filthy sidewalks, passing rows of derelict houses which had been all but destroyed by bums and vandals and yet other houses, equally ravaged but nevertheless occupied by people who fought a losing battle against heat, cold, rain, noise, vermin, filth, and just plain despair.

"This," Brian said with only faint irony, "is my constituency. These are the people I represent."

"But there's almost no one here," Tracy said. "Oh, yeah, there's people in that house, but we passed three houses and they're all empty. And all those on the other side of the street are boarded up."

"That's my point," Brian said. "There used to be people here. It wasn't much but it *was* a neighborhood. My neighborhood. It's where I grew up."

"But what happened? Where'd they all go?" Tracy asked.

"What happened is what's happening all over town. What's happening in your neighborhood too. That's why I was there. Remember all those smart-ass things you were saying? OK, you listen and maybe you'll learn something," he said severely.

Tracy grinned and ducked her head and held tightly to his arm.

"This neighborhood," he went on, "had the guts torn right out of it. That's what's going down around here. Going down all over town. A few years ago when there was all that commotion, it looked like maybe things would change. Not just for black people but for everybody in this city who'd been ripped off or pushed around or just born unlucky. I'm talking about all the hillbillies and Polacks and poor dumb rednecks who come up here looking for jobs and a place to live. But it didn't happen. For a while there it looked like out of all that anger, some kind of feeling was stirring, feeling for each other. Now–" He shrugged.

"It's hard to feel for somebody else," Tracy said softly, "when you're feeling so low you can barely keep yourself up."

"Keep yourself *up?*" he looked at her keenly. "Or out? Because that's what you really mean, isn't it? What you want is out? Far out? Soon out? For good out?"

Stung, Tracy picked her head up and glared at him. "You're damn right I want out!" she said. "And I'm going to get out! Do you blame me?"

"I believe you," he said blandly, ignoring her challenge. "Trouble, is, most people around here don't stand a chance of going with you. They aren't going to get out. So somebody's got to give them some hope, give them a hand. Pick them up enough so they can help themselves."

"And that someone is you, is that it? Bold St. Brian, your friendly neighborhood messiah!"

He laughed easily and pleasantly. "I been called worse. Seriously, you start with what you got. This is what I got so this is where I start. I've done the uptown bit Tracy, with the conservative threads and the bright young lawyer routine. They work on you, they suck you in until you're so ashamed of where you came from that you can't even remember it. And then they've got you, Tracy, bought you for a song. The men patting you on the shoulder and telling you the latest dirty jokes and pouring more booze than you can drink. And the chicks giving you the eye and letting you know you can have it morning, night or afternoon. And the worst thing is, it's unconscious. They aren't cynical. They're not even aware of what they're doing. But they're doing it. They're pulling out your claws, your fangs, turning you into a pussycat. And then they've got you where you can't do yourself or anybody else any more good."

"Whew!" she said, grinning. "You do get worked up, don't you."

He glared at her fiercely for a moment, the heat of passion still upon him, but then broke into his easy smile. "OK, you wanted to know where I lived, what was happening. Now you know. I'm a political garbage collector. I pick up other people's lost causes."

"Alone," Tracy said pointedly.

"Not intentionally. But as it happens–yes, mostly alone."

"Who was the guy in *Man of La Mancha*, the one with the windmills and the impossible dream?"

"Don Quixote," he said, looking up at her. "Let me tell you something about this alone bit, Tracy. The point is, I am never truly alone. Because I'm working *with* people, *for* people. Only time you're really alone is when you're working just for number one."

They walked on in silence through the late afternoon sun.

When they got to her door Brian embraced her. Tracy was shocked at his obvious strength and appreciative of his gentleness. But she couldn't–or wouldn't?–respond. Something held her back, something fearful, unresolved. Whatever is was, it nagged. She put her hands on his chest, enjoying the solid feeling of him, wanting and yet not wanting to extend that touch.

"It's been a great day, Brian. A different kind of day for me–but I want it to end now, OK?"

He nodded. There was nothing more to say and, wisely, he didn't say it.

He started to turn away and then halted, one foot on the step. "Tracy," he said, "is there–I mean–" He faltered and stopped. "Forget it," he grinned, waving his hand.

"The answer," she said levelly, looking into his eyes, "is no. There isn't."

He waved again and went down the stairs.

Three

On Monday morning Tracy came out of the employees' elevator and threaded her way through the corridors approaching the display department where she worked. When she neared Linda Evans's office, she was startled to see several fashion models, all of them white, beautiful, and fully made-up, lounging around the doorway of one of the display department workrooms. Coming through the open doorway she heard a—by now—familiar irritated voice.

"Try to look surprised, darling. Shocked. Like you've just been balled by your dentist."

Both the voice and the rattlesnake disposition belonged to Sean McAvoy.

The room in which he was working looked like a surrealist's version of Judgment Day. Nude mannequins, both whole and in disassembled parts, hung from the walls and ceilings. Arms, legs, pelvic basins—

minus pubic hair, of course—torsos without navels, bosoms without nipples, bald heads, graceful hands, and ever-staring eyes. It was like a humanoid delicatessen. And that wasn't all. Elsewhere around the room, in corners and on the walls and ceilings were leftover props from former window displays, some of them real, culled from junkyards and antique shops, others fabricated by skilled craftsmen so that they had a two-dimensional reality. Half a butter churn, for example, made out of textured plastic, complete with plastic rust stains and wormholes. A whole ox yoke, half a guitar, mason jars, high bicycles, a stuffed monkey on top of a plastic hurdy-gurdy, part of a grape arbor, an enormous brass samovar, and one-third of a liberty bell.

And somehow, in the middle of all this, Sean McAvoy had had a seamless paper background rigged and was taking Polaroid shots of models making lewd advances to something that looked a hayrick.

McAvoy, with his slender, nervy intensity, was in some ways the strangest figure in this room. He seemed not only to be undaunted by his surroundings but in some strange way stimulated. It was as if some insane or perverse streak in his nature fed and was nourished by all of this bizarre visual impact. He moved stiffly, quickly in stiff-legged hops and jumps like a cicada in an old fatique jacket. He barely addressed the models, signalling to them with knifelike gestures of his bony hands, dismissing them as soon as he'd completed a roll, motioning the next one on the scene without even taking his eye from the viewfinder of his camera. Tracy thought he must be in a kind of trance and she was awed by it. Soundlessly she withdrew, fearful of what might happen if his eye fell on her. It was as though she'd become a child again and had wandered into a fairy story. With one stroke the wicked witch might turn her into stone.

A few hours later, just as she pushed herself away from her desk and was about to go out for lunch, Aunt Florence bustled in carrying an old shopping bag.

"Hey, girl," she called out, "I think you got you a winner."

"Oh! Aunt Florence. You did it!"

"You didn't think I'd come all the way over here just to say I didn't do it, did you?"

"No–I only meant–you know!" Tracy gave her aunt a hug.

Florence pulled a tissue-wrapped package out of the shopping bag, stripped off the paper, and then held the dress up for Tracy to see.

"Oh, my God!" Tracy exulted. "Did I do *that!*"

"Hell, no," Florence said, "I did that. But you thought of it. Ain't you going to put it on?"

Tracy grabbed the dress and stepped inside a small curtained changing booth normally used by models. A few moments later she emerged with the dress on. Florence threw up her hands.

"Sen-sational!" she said. "I mean, that's fantastic, honey."

"Mmm," Tracy said grimly, looking at herself in the full-length mirror. "It really is good. And of course you made the thing fit better than my skin. You're a goddamned wizard, Aunt Florrie. Wait, I've got to comb my hair differently." She tugged furiously at her neat hair, pulling it severely all to one side.

"How's that, better?" she asked her aunt.

"Dynamite!" Sean McAvoy said, clicking his camera even as she turned. "Go. Again," he said, as Tracy began to strike one pose after the next. She frowned, she pouted, she threw back her head and laughed raucously. And for an instant she was really enjoying herself. This was a feeling she hadn't anticipated. She'd always designed clothes for "other" people to wear. And it never occurred to her what pleasure there was in being stared at, photographed in the clothes she had designed.

"Now fan the skirt out," Sean ordered. "Twirl around. Move it, move it, come on, damn it, dance. Let me see the legs, the thighs. Good. Terrific. Hey, you're a pro, aren't you?"

"Hunh?" Tracy said, coming back to reality again.

"Don't hunh me—you're a pro and you know it."

"But I—I never modeled anything before. What's more, I don't want to."

"Don't want to. Turn. Put that right arm out. All the way out. Good. Come on, Miss Chambers, what's with this modesty number?"

"I'm not modest," Tracy said, "it's just that I think being a live coat hanger is for dummies."

"Anything is for dummies when they can't do it right," Sean McAvoy said, "and that includes modeling. But when you're good at something, I mean really super, the way you are—then you transform that activity into something special. You dig what I'm telling you."

"Yeah, I dig," Tracy said grudgingly. He had scored a point. "But my thing isn't modeling clothes, it's designing them. This, for example. What you see me wearing."

"Hey, no kidding!" Sean said, "you designed that?"

"Well, me and my tailor shop over there." Tracy grinned, indicating Aunt Florence. "Florence Hampton," she said, "this is Sean McAvoy."

"How do you do, Florence," Sean said pleasantly. "I'm really impressed with that gown. But there's one problem."

"What's that," Tracy asked quickly.

"I mean aside from wearing it so beautifully," Sean said with a tinge of sarcasm, "which you've already told me you aren't really interested in doing—what the hell are you going to do with it?"

"Why, sell it, of course," Tracy said. "This is part of my spring line."

"Part of your spring line? Hey, that's terrific. I mean it's really great to have a spring line with that kind of thing going for it. What about the other numbers in the line?"

"Well, they haven't—um—been manufactured yet."

"And you're going to market that line right here in Chicago, right?" he persisted.

"Well, of course, you think I was going to go down to Peoria?"

"You pitiful little dope. This *is* Peoria!" he said.

"There's nothing wrong with Chicago," Tracy said hotly, wondering if she really meant it.

"Nothing wrong with it that a ticket to Europe wouldn't cure," Sean said.

"Europe!" He'd taken Tracy by surprise. "That's halfway across the world."

"Oh, I know it," Sean said wistfully. "Boy, do I know it. You know something, honey—you'd really love it in Rome. And they'd love you."

"Oh? Why's that?"

"Because in Rome, Miss Chambers, they drink their coffee out of pretty things. They don't send their pretty things out to get their coffee. Do you dig what I'm tellin' you?"

Tracy laughed. "Yeah," she said, "I can dig it."

Florence, who had been watching this exchange and who could tell that there was something about McAvoy which attracted Tracy, had nevertheless a gut feeling that there was something dangerous here. She grumbled an old woolly-head kind of grumble, a pose which she normally didn't permit herself. "This here chile don' know nothin' 'bout no Rome," she growled, "she jus' a simple 'Murcan girl."

"I didn't think she did know anything about Rome, ma'am," Sean said, "and that's the very quality they'd like most about her."

"I don't get you, Mr. McAvoy," Tracy said coolly.

"Yes you do," Sean said, "you may be innocent but you're not *that* innocent. You know what I'm talking about—freshness, youth. You're unspoiled, untutored. You've got a sheen about you."

Tracy was about to reply but clamped her mouth shut when her boss, Linda Evans, walked in.

"What, may I ask," Linda said in a high fluting voice, "is going on here?" She addressed the question to Tracy and obviously expected her to reply and just as obviously wasn't going to accept that reply.

"Tell you how it is, Miz Evans," Sean drawled a kind of country shitkicker drawl totally out of keeping with his hip background. "I been lookin' at these here little gals for two days now, tryin' to make a decent photo layout and I ain't seen one who's a patch on this li'l gal. Now," he said, quickly shifting gears, "you can say that she isn't a model. But I don't care what she does for a living, Miss Chambers *is* a model. What's more, she's the model for this particular layout. Do you read me?"

Tracy shuddered at his calm insolence and Aunt Florence, sensing that she was out of her depth, tried to make herself small.

"Mr. McAvoy," Linda Evans said softly, "I'm sorry, but what you're suggesting is totally out of the question."

Sean's reply was just as soft, just as treacherous. "Would you be questioning my judgment, Miss Evans? Are you telling me my business?"

Linda Evans faltered. His calm was too much for her. "No," she said hastily, "of course I'm not. It's just that–" a pleading note entered her voice. "The fact is, Mr. McAvoy, the agency we're dealing with–they maintain a conservative policy. I mean, they have national distribution to think of, and there are considerations that you and I are free to ignore–"

"What *is* all of this shit, Miss Evans?" Sean McAvoy exploded.

She stiffened as if he'd struck her but regained her composure almost at once. "My hands are tied, Mr. McAvoy. And you needn't try to make me feel guilty for the instructions which have been passed on to me. These aren't my notions of how to run a business. On the other hand, it isn't my business."

And with that she turned and left the room.

Sean McAvoy laughed silently and finally let out a long sigh. "OK, Miss Chambers," he said, "do you still want to know why I prefer Rome to Chicago?"

"No," she said very softly, "I think I get the message."

Sean McAvoy slung his camera over his shoulder, gestured goodbye to Aunt Florence and to Tracy, then bethought himself. "What time do they let you out of bondage?" he asked.

"Five o'clock."

"OK, meet me out front at five oh five and I'll buy you a drink."

"But–"

She didn't finish the sentence. He was gone.

At quitting time Tracy managed to make it down the stairs without bumping into Linda Evans. In fact, she hadn't even seen her boss all afternoon. She was grateful for that because she had no idea what she'd have been able to say to that fearsome lady. It did not occur to her that her boss might have avoided her for the same reason. In any case, Tracy found Sean McAvoy waiting for her in front of the store. As usual, he was wearing his beat-up army fatigue jacket, carrying a Nikon over his shoulder and an air of infinite weariness. He was an intriguing figure, so slender as to appear frail, yet very strong when in action. His clothing made him appear something of a hippie, yet his glance was full of direction and total authority. She found herself responding to him with something like awe and pity at the same time. Strange! But intriguing.

Later when they were seated over drinks at a nearby bar she found herself apologizing for Linda Evans. "You were pretty hard on her, you know, it wasn't her fault."

"Hard on her!" Sean McAvoy said. "Dear innocent Tracy. I wasn't hard on that old bitch. If I wanted, I could have had her job. I could have her ass out of there in five minutes if I'd wanted."

"You have that much power?" Tracy said.

"It's simple, Tracy. All I have to do is call up the general manager of Marshall Field and let him know that I'm planning a feature story for *Ms.* or *Cosmopolitan* or *Vogue* or *Mademoiselle*–on guess what? Racial prejudice in the country's largest department stores. How long do you think your Linda Evans would last?"

"Could you actually *do* a story like that?"

"Jesus, Tracy, you really are a hick. At the prices I get, they'd fall all over themselves to get a story from me because I'd offer to sell it to them at half price! Because it's a pet of mine, a passion. You really don't know much, do you?"

"No," Tracy said. "It's true, I don't know much." She thought for a moment and then added, "But one thing I do know, getting back to Linda Evans, that is. I can see why she doesn't want a black girl modeling her clothes. I mean, how many black faces do you see in *Vogue* or *Harper's Bazaar?*"

Sean didn't answer her. He was tapping the bar top with a plastic mixing rod, concentrating, frowning. "Hey, I've got it," he said. "I'll do a whole fashion layout down in the ghetto. I mean the heavy bad ghetto, the worst there is. Kids, dogs, laundry, crap, graffiti, winos, the works."

"You're talking," Tracy said sweetly, "about the place where I live."

He laughed. "Terrific. Now—can you see these lily-white dummies with their tight little teeny-bopper asses up against those grimy walls and all those gorgeous clothes with FUCK and SUCK painted in letters yay high? Fantastic!"

"Oh, it'd be fantastic all right." Tracy laughed along with his joke. "Of course it might end up with everybody in the hospital, too, you know."

"That's just it!" Sean said keenly, slapping the bar so that other people jumped. Tracy peered at him, suddenly realizing that this wasn't some sort of joke-fantasy. He was serious. "That's the quality I'm looking for. Danger! Don't look at me that way. I know what I'm doing. I've covered as many war stories as fashion stories—where the hell do you think I got my experience? As a combat photographer. And that's the quality I've never been able to get into a fashion layout. Jesus, it'd be terrific, Tracy. And you're going to help me."

"Me! Well–" Tracy was frightened but she was also flattered. His enthusiasm swept her reserve away. "If you think I can help you, you ought to know what you're doing."

"OK," Sean said, forgetting that whole idea at once. "Now all we have to do is figure out how to get you to Rome. Now let me think about this a moment–"

Tracy couldn't believe him. "Hey–" she said, but he ignored her, so deep in thought that he almost appeared to be falling asleep.

"You-hoo, Mr. McAvoy," Tracy called, "remember me?" and this time he grunted in her direction.

"I'm assuming," he muttered, "that you really are serious about becoming a designer. I don't mean some little schlock designer but for real, right. The top?"

"Oh, am I ever," Tracy said reverently. "Mister, you'll never know how I feel about designing clothes. I like to think about them, draw them, feel them, wear them, my head is so popping with ideas about clothes I sometimes think my mind will blow. And let me tell you something else: I'm bound and determined to make it. The top or bust! I know, I know, everybody *says* that. But I *mean* it. And I'm not just sitting around with my finger in my ear waiting and praying for somebody to believe in me. *I* believe in me! And that's all the believing I need. Am I coming through to you?"

"Oh, yes you are, Tracy," Sean said admiringly. "That's the kind of gutsy talk I need to hear. Because you've got a tough road to travel. But that's my whole point. You've *got* to travel it. You've got to get out of this Mickey Mouse town. Christ almighty, you're more of an oddball here than I am! If you can design things like the one I saw you with today, you're as out of place as an orchid in a butcher shop. You've got to split, Tracy, and fast. Before they get to you."

She stared at him, both thrilled and alarmed. There

was no mistaking the passionate intensity of his argument. His sincerity was beyond question. It was the argument itself that she suddenly found frightening. Leave? Now? And where to? Sure, she'd dreamed all her life of going to New York, San Francisco, even Paris—but dreaming was one thing. Contemplating it as an immediate reality was something else again. And intimidating.

Sensing her frightened mood, Sean sought to reassure her. "Hey, let's just relax," he said, patting her hand. "How about you and I finding some Italian restaurant. The pasta will be lousy but I'll pretend that it's good and we'll enjoy ourselves."

"Oh!" Tracy said, glancing at her watch, "I can't do that. Sorry. But I've got a date."

McAvoy's face creased. He wasn't used to being refused. "A date?" he said lightly. "You mean you haven't got time for one more drink?"

"I can't," Tracy said, climbing off her chair. "I'm afraid I'm late now."

"Well," he said, smiling a trifle too broadly, "I wouldn't want to interfere with a case of true love. It is a case of true love, isn't it?"

Tracy suddenly found this interrogation making her uncomfortable, yet she couldn't bring herself to be rude. "It's just a date." She attempted to be light about it, and then seeing his face fall, she added, "Listen, we'll really knock 'em out with that fashion layout you were talking about. I mean, you will. It's a terrific idea."

"Yeah, right," Sean said glumly, "terrific idea. See you."

She waved and was gone.

It was a relief to be back in Brian's presence. The restaurant where they sat was a quiet, neighborhood sort of place, decent without pretension. Brian filled her glass with wine but she'd had two martinis with Sean McAvoy, and was so unaccustomed to their affect that she tottered on the edge of drunkenness. Brian, if he noticed, didn't remark on it and she was relieved that he didn't press her about being late. Perhaps that was the thing about him that she liked the most. He didn't press. For one thing, he was so full of his own plans and his own projects that he talked on and on through dinner without requiring more from her than an occasional sign she was following the conversation. And that too she found comforting. Because there was a part of her mind that was troubled and made uneasy by Sean McAvoy's behavior even though she couldn't put her finger on exactly what it was.

One thing that gave her cause for alarm was his intention to shoot a fashion layout in the ghetto. She talked about this to Brian and expressed her fears. Did he think there would be trouble? He thought this over carefully.

"Could be," he said finally. "Doesn't necessarily mean there will be. A lot depends on how he handles himself. A lot of folks will really resent it if he gives out the wrong kind of vibes. I mean, if he comes on like the slick-talking liberal—'My dear, I know how you must suffer'—he's liable to get his ass in a sling. Because he *don't* know how these folks suffer. And never will know or can know. So if he doesn't lie but just handles himself in a straight forward way, I'd say nobody's gonna bother him. How about you?" he said.

"How about me what?" Tracy asked.

"I mean," Brian said, "how do you feel about this? What kind of feelings does it give you—going into the ghetto with a bunch of two-hundred-dollar dresses, draping them on these white chippies and taking pictures of them standing around like they don't even know they're standing on a pile of garbage? What does that do to you?"

Tracy frowned. "I guess," she said slowly, "I get two kinds of feelings about that. Now don't get mad at me, Brian," she cautioned.

"I won't get mad," he said. "It's your feelings we're talking about, not mine."

"OK," Tracy said, "the two kinds of feelings I get

are these: bad, because I think there's something kind of rotten about taking these pictures in the heart of all this misery and then sending them back to New York where they will be laid out in some fancy fashion magazine so a lot of chicks can look at those clothes and say, "My, my, isn't that daring! Look at that blond girl with her nipples showing right through that blouse—and in the ghetto too! I mean, my dear, it's so with-it!" She finished her own exaggerated imitation and made a wry face to indicate her disgust. "Of course that riles me, Brian. It has to. But I get good feelings too. First of all, about working with McAvoy. This guy has to be some kind of genius—it's a cinch he's number one in the business. And that means something to me, Brian, can you understand that? Number one—I don't care what it is: brain surgeon, lawyer, number one hooker, number one *anything!* It's a kick to work with someone who's at the top."

"I hear you," Brian said, "and I dig what you're saying."

"Another thing," Tracy went on, "the idea is basically exciting, visually, I mean. It may be hard for you to follow this, you're not an artist—but think of the textures! We're talking about jagged brick and rusted iron railings and broken wooden fences and shattered glass—all those sharp points and rough edges, right? OK, and in contrast to that, we put all these sleek fabrics and flowing designs and delicate willowy girls, light colors in the midst of all that dirt and grit. Do you see what I mean? You see the kind of aesthetic tension that comes out of a juxtaposition like that?"

"Juxtaposition! Hey, you comin' on strong, girl." He laughed amiably and Tracy had to join in.

"OK, OK," she said, "I know I sound like a first-year art student, but I just wanted to show you that each—what? trade? profession? has its own inner rules and organization. With politics it's the same, right?"

"With politics there's only one rule," Brian said. "get elected. And when you're elected, get reelected."

"Come on, Brian, be serious," Tracy pleaded.

"You think I'm not being serious?" he said.

She looked at him and then her expression softened and turned fond. "You know, one of the things I like about you," she said, "you never really tease me or put me down. I'm so used to that, I suppose, that I'm always suspecting you of doing it. But you don't. And I appreciate that."

"And I appreciate your appreciating that," he said, "and I also appreciate that you haven't finished your veal parmigiana and I'd better do it for you so you won't get too fat to model those pretty clothes you design, OK?"

An hour later, tired, replete, they arrived at Tracy's door. Tracy had taken another glass of wine before leaving the restaurant and her head now drooped on its stem, her nose rubbing slightly against Brian's face. Ever so gently, he tipped her chin up and kissed her, softly, tenderly at first, and then, enfolding her, he was more demanding. She felt herself fitting into every contour of his body and it was a very long time before a sense of time returned to her. He was speaking, his mouth warm against her ear.

"Keys," he said. "Keys. You must have twenty-nine different locks on that door and that means you've got to have twenty-nine different keys."

"Oh," she said finally, reaching into her purse. It was an effort. She felt so comfortable pressed against him that she never wanted to move again.

She felt his arm reach out and unlock the door and she automatically put out her hand to receive the keys. But he didn't put them in her hand, he slipped them in his pocket. "I'll take care of those," he muttered. And then she felt herself being lifted off the floor. "I'll take care of this bundle too," he said, carrying her inside and shutting the door with his elbow.

"Be careful," she warned softly, afraid that this broad-shouldered man with his heavy burden might knock over a lamp or break a vase. But he moved as easily and as lightly as a giant cat, not bothering to put on the lights and carrying her expertly to the bedroom. Then he laid her on the bed.

Almost at once, now that she was fully horizontal, the wine rushed to her brain. "Brian," she whimpered, "oh, Brian."

"What is it?" he asked, sitting on the edge of the bed beside her.

"Oh, Brian, I don't want to disappoint you!"

"You couldn't disappoint me, honey," he whispered.

"It's just–I–I'm afraid–I'm drunk, Brian. Too much wine. Too much–"

"Ssh!" he said, "don't worry about it. You just lie there and leave the driving to me, OK?"

Dimly she felt his hands move on her, on her legs, her thighs, her breast. He lifted her and opened her dress, then laid her down again. Expertly he removed her panty hose, and just as expertly drew his fingers lightly across her flat little belly to see if there was any quiver. She felt a delicious involuntary spasm shake her and then he was gone.

"Wh-where–where?" she mumbled.

A moment later he was back and she felt an icy cloth on her face and neck. The shock almost made her cry out. But an instant later she was grateful for the restorative aid of that cold damp cloth. He moved it down over her breasts and then over her belly, gently parting her thighs so that warmest part of her body would be cooled as well. Then, tossing the cloth aside, he gently toweled her dry. The combination of that cool dampness followed by the rough towel made her skin come alive as if she'd just leaped out of a swimming pool. All sense of dizziness was replaced now by another kind of feeling, a deep aching longing to be touched gently, tenderly, and then more roughly, savagely.

And she found that her longing was excited by his smooth warm hands which touched and kneaded her nipples and the cup of her small breast. She felt his breath and then his warm tongue on her nipples, raising them up, turning them harder than she thought she could stand. And his hand, moving down over her belly and between her legs, grasped her firmly, urgently, causing her to arch her body up to meet him. She gasped as his strong fingers parted her damp flesh, seeking the wetness, encouraging, urging, so that she felt herself opening wider and wider, pressing more hungrily against him, until, gasping with a pleasure she had never known before, she felt his great stiff cock inching and urging, inching and urging, settling deeper and deeper inside her until he commanded her entire being, causing her to rise and fall, rise and fall, until she felt herself wanting to open so wide, to take him so deeply, to seize him with such sweet violence that she cried out in pain and joy and love and exultation. "Oh!" she cried. "Oh! Oh!"

And she heard his low, single answer, "Yes!"

Sometime later, when they were quiet again in the darkness, she smiled against his face and said softly, "Well, I guess we've got us a beginning of something, haven't we?"

"For which," he said "thank God!"

He sounded so serious, so solemn, that Tracy had to giggle. He didn't join her laugh, however. She felt, without quite being able to see his face in the darkness, that his expression was very straight. As usual, Brian had meant exactly what he'd said.

Tracy somehow got herself onto the subway in the morning, but she was in such a state of conflicted feelings that she was almost catatonic. Numbly, she stared for long seconds at her feet, fearing that she might have forgotten to put on her shoes. It was as if she were being buffeted by two enormous and opposing tides. There was no question about the one tide—that was LOVE! Clear, bright, unquestioned, and unbelievably warm. She felt for Brian what she had felt for no other man since she'd had her long teenage crush. And this was no crush. She was a young woman and, with her hardscrabble ghetto background, wiser than most. Her eyes were wide open and there he stood, squarely in the center of her gaze—bold and beautiful

So much for that tide.

And the other—she sighed. Much harder to define, except to say that it was contrary to, the opposite of, and a mortal threat to the first. Call it, she decided, *flight*. Today, for example, this very morning, she would be working with Sean McAvoy—and a part of her mind responded with instant excitement and enthusiasm. But where would this lead her? The answer was clear: away! And what's more, she *wanted* away. Sean talked of Rome. Yeah, yeah, yeah, she told herself derisively. Promises, promises. But the fact remained that she was aiming to get away, working, aching to get away. And if Sean McAvoy was useful as a tool then she'd damn well use him. And be used, she added, fiercely.

So there it was. Pow! right in the kisser. The kisser! She smiled at her own choice of words. Because the feel of Brian's kisses still weighed on her mouth, on her eyelids, and on all the warm secret places of her body. Most important, she felt them imprinted on her soul. She'd been kissed before and loved before, passionately, tenderly, and she'd responded in kind. But never before had anyone gone past the delicate but terribly tough fibers of her last defense barrier. Never had she opened herself so completely, made herself so vulnerable, so naked. A wound had opened inside her, infinitely sweet. It would be a long time—if ever—before it healed.

Brian was here, now, she told herself. And she? She was all in the future. All looking ahead—and away. Brian was roots. Brian was confrontation. And all she wanted was out.

"Why," she moaned, "Jesus-God *why* does life have to be so complicated?"

And the city-weary voice of an old subway rider answered her, "I don't know, lady—why don't you write a letter to Mayor Daley?"

Astonished, she lifted her head, identified the voice as coming from an old man sitting across the aisle who indicated the open doors of the subway car. Apparently, it had been stalled in this position for some minutes, standing at the empty station platform.

Her platform! She gave a small shriek and dashed out of the car. And then proceeded to double up with laughter like a madwoman. "Why does life have to be so complicated?" she said aloud, and became hysterical all over again.

Setting up in the ghetto attracted a crowd almost from the start. As Tracy knew and had warned Sean it would. There were an awful lot of people without jobs, without homes, without purpose, who collected like flies at the scene of even the most minor incident. Anything, she explained, to relieve the boredom of their lives. And this was no minor incident. It was like an invasion—from the Planet Uptown.

There were tripods with lights, reflectors, parabolic light diffusers, electrical cable, satchels, cartons, clothes racks. There were models, a dozen of them, uniformly slim and willowy, blonde, brunette, red-haired, and all of them white. There were hairdressers, seamstresses, grips, electricians, a catering truck, a dressing-room trailer, armed security men, as well as a unit of riot police and frantic assistants, male and female. And in the center of all this stood Sean McAvoy, a somewhat aging god Pan in a fatigue jacket, causing everyone to hop to his tune.

The target area of Sean McAvoy's cameras was a two-story frame house which looked as if it had been lifted off the ground in a tornado, blown to bits, and reassembled by that same tornado and returned to earth. It seemed to lean in three directions at the same time. Windows were boarded up, fire had burned a patch through the roof, walls were covered with vintage graffiti. And on the two porches, upper and lower, Sean had positioned glamorously clothed models, interspersing them with free-lance models from the community.

These blacks, some of them ancient, some of them skinny kids, seemed so far not to have taken an emotional position about this event or their participation in it. Their faces were neutral, inscrutable. Only to a trained eye, such as Brian Walker's, were there any signs of danger. From a vantage point on the periphery of this whole scene, the rusty remains of a chain link fence, he shook his head with disgust—and doubt. Street-wise, sensitive to the mercurial nature of his disenfranchised brothers, he knew that their placid nature could be transformed in an instant, that they could —without warning and just for the hell of it—go on a bloody vicious rampage that would not end until they were handcuffed or clubbed into immobility. Thinking about this possibility caused Brian to shudder. And it deeply dismayed him that these poor helpless misfits and unfortunates, some of them drugged, some of them juiced, some of them stupefied by too much desperation, might suddenly be kindled by a chance spark and so go to their own destruction.

Looking around him casually so as not to give alarm to those who stood nearest him, Brian scanned the adjacent streets and empty lots and confirmed what he had feared. The police department had quietly mobilized a reserve riot force including a mobile tear-gas generator and a high-powered water pumper so that in the event of trouble they would be able to move quickly and with force.

Tracy, of course, in her frantic rush to do Sean's bidding and even to anticipate his machine-gun commands, had no thoughts for anything but the job at hand. She had not even noticed that Brian was standing near until he actually reached out and touched her one time as she trotted by.

"Hey, lady," he said, "what's goin' down?"

"Oh!" she gasped in surprise. "I thought you were some—some—"

"Some what? Black rapist? Mugger? You gettin' kinda mixed up, aren't you?"

"No, dummy," she said easily, not noticing his underlying tension, "I just thought, you know, somebody hittin' on me . . ."

"That's what I'm here for, all right," Brian said. "I ought to hit you right on top of the head. Do you realize this little outing in the park might blow up all over you?"

"Oh, come on, Brian, not now," she pleaded. "We break for lunch in about ten minutes and you can lecture me then, OK?"

But he didn't quite let go of her arm. Leveling a glance at Sean McAvoy, he asked, "That him? The great white hope?"

"Cut it out, will you, Brian?" Tracy was stung. "No cheap shots."

"OK, cool," he mumbled, smiling vaguely and keeping his eyes on Sean. "Looks like he knows what he's doing. God knows, he's busy enough."

"He's like that all the time," Tracy said, unable to keep an admiring tone out of her voice and wishing she had. "Never stops moving. He's like a ballet dancer. And don't get any ideas; he's straight. At least I think he is. He used to be a combat photographer."

"He's got guts all right," Brian conceded, "coming down here with this whole setup. He might just find himself in combat again." He tilted his head and indicated some of the young bloods who were standing nearby. On their faces Tracy could read a peculiar expression. They were watching a tall and unusually well-endowed model lean into a pose over the upper porch railing, her attractive breasts almost falling out of her fragmentary dress. And what bothered Tracy was that their expression was not one of mere lust or excitement. They looked, she thought, as if they'd like to take that model apart like a child's toy, just to see how it worked.

"Uh, Brian," she murmured, "is there going to be trouble?"

He shrugged. "I hope not. But there could be."

"Can you do anything about it?" she begged. "Please."

"You mean can I? or will I?"

She was about to answer him when Sean called her imperiously, "Tracy! On the double!"

Tracy spun away and Brian watched her run to Sean's side. She tilted her head as he spoke intimately in her ear, gesturing at the same time, pointing to the house and to various models and bystanders.

"That old woman," Sean was saying, "the one with the cataracts. I've got to have her in this next scene. Tell her—no, don't tell her I'll pay her. That'll start a riot. Tell her I've got a bottle of muscatel in my trailer. She can come by later and get a drink."

"Gee, Brian," Tracy hesitated. The old woman looked so fragile, so bewildered—and at the same time, so dignified.

"Go on, hop!" he said, patting her on the ass, "this is the big time, kid. Get with it."

Brian's eyes narrowed as he took in this vignette. He knew enough about Tracy to know that if it had been anybody else who had so freely caressed her behind, she'd have backhanded him in front of this whole audience. Her restraint made him thoughtful. He was still more thoughtful when he saw how quickly effective she was in winning assent from the old woman and guiding her, shepherding her into the picture so that Sean rewarded Tracy with a huge, gestured kiss.

A moment later, motioned out of the scene by a dictatorial Sean, who rapped out commands as he aimed and clicked, Tracy came back to stand near Brian.

"Tell me something," Brian said, "you get paid extra for letting him grab you on the ass?"

"Oh, don't pull that jealousy number on me, baby," Tracy protested, "you *know* where I'm at."

"Maybe," he said glumly. "What about them? What about that old lady and those others. How much they getting for this?"

"Uh, how—I—don't know," she said.

"How about the models. They get paid, don't they? This is their business, right?"

"About sixty an hour," Tracy said, "for most of them. A few—that one there, and the girl standing above her, get seventy. And there's one girl, I think she's changing now, who gets a hundred."

"An hour," Brian said ponderously.

"It sounds like a lot. Of course, they don't work regularly—"

"And the old lady nothing," Brian persisted. "And that little kid with his arm around that white girl's waist. Nothing for him either. That's a cute shot, isn't it. Skinny little kid with his arm around her waist, like she's so sophisticated and he's such a little bitty thing, so innocent. Shee-itttt!" he spat. "That little kid was never innocent. He had his innocence ripped off him the moment he was born. You want me to tell you what's going on in that kid's mind? Want me to tell you what he's fixing to do with his other hand?"

Tracy was starting to get unstrung. "Damn it, Brian," she warned. "Do you have to be so hostile? Do you? It's my job. I'm trying to do my job. And it isn't politics, it's fashion. A different world."

"There are no different worlds, baby," Brian said evenly. "Only one. And everything in it is political."

"For you!" she said fiercely. "Not for me. All of this—" she gestured. "It may be make-believe to you, but it's real to me. It's the world of fashion and the world of art. Fantasy is what it's all about."

"Your world, right?" Brian said. "With just a little color thrown in from my world. A little dark stain. To give it character, right?"

"I can't believe we're having this fight," Tracy said grimly, putting her hands over her ears. "I just can't believe it, not after last night."

"Yeah, well—" and then Brian broke off. Sean McAvoy had turned his back on his models and was snapping pictures of an overwrought Tracy who was trying, by placing her hands over her ears, to keep the sound of dissension from echoing in her mind. After three or four fast shots, Sean winked at Brian and then reversed himself, going back to his models again.

"Looks like he must be pretty high on you," Brian said, indicating Sean. "He offered to take you up to his darkroom yet? Or don't he use that word 'dark' room? Maybe he calls it 'light' room."

"Listen," Tracy said through clenched teeth, "if you don't cut out this childishness—you're insulting me, you're insulting yourself. Will you do me a favor, please, Brian—let it ride till lunchtime, OK?"

Before Brian could answer, Sean called, "Tracy! Lacy Tracy, get over here, will you. I've gotta get out of here, got a plane to catch. Move it, girl!"

"Uh, you better do like the man says, sister," Brian said, slurring his speech sarcastically, "look like he needs hisself another nigger!"

"WHAT did you say!" Tracy gasped.

"Tracy!" Sean called again. "Knock off the chatter, will you!"

"Look," Brian said quickly, "I'm sorry, OK. I got hot. But I don't like you taking part in this giant rip-off. It's not just a black-white thing, it's a money thing—"

"What rip-off?" Tracy challenged. "What in the hell are you talking about?"

"You mean you honestly don't know," Brian said scornfully. "You can't see that this whole damn thing is a rip-off? a little number for the power elite? They're using this mess," he gestured, "this whole damn slum just to promote business! For profit. *His* profit. The slick smart-ass photographer, right? Darling of the fashion world? And what about the people making those threads, selling those threads. Who gets the profit? That half-blind old lady there? You! Rip-off, dummy. Wake up!" Brian's contempt was naked now.

"It's my job!" Tracy protested. "Fashion is what I do. I don't expect you to understand it. Just respect it."

"And this is what you want, right? This is where you're headed?" Brian bored in relentlessly.

"Working with the best? Hell, yes. Class is class, you admitted that yourself—"

Brian threw up his hands. "Baby, you're so right. I don't understand. I don't understand the trip you're on. I don't understand bringing these little chicks down here to wear these clothes. I don't understand—and *they* don't understand." He gestured at the wooden features of black bystanders. "They don't understand it because it has no meaning. For them!"

"Well, I understand it. It has meaning for me!"

"Oh, you—well, now, that's different, isn't it. I mean, if it's OK by your standards, then it's OK, period. Right?"

"Are you forgetting who I *am*, Brian?" Tracy hissed. "Are you forgetting that I come from here too, that I have as much right to like what I like and think what I think as you have?"

"Think? No," Brian said. "Hustle, maybe. You're hustling all right, hustling your way out of here so you can forget all about it. And once you're a thousand miles away it won't exist anymore. Congratulations, it's a neat trick if you can make it work. I can't."

"I'll tell you what I can't forget," Tracy said venomously. "I can't forget all the times I've been told where I can't go, what I can't do, what I can't even think, for Christ's sake. I've been told what I can't hope and what I can't dream and what I can't work for and believe and laugh at. I've been told it by white. I've been told it by black. I've been told not to push too hard and not to talk too soft. I've been told I can't even be myself! And the last person I want to hear that kinda talk from—is you!"

"Does it matter?" Brian said tensely. "I mean I know we made it and all last night. But does it matter what I say?"

"Tracy! For Christ's sake!" Sean called out in a temper.

"Brian—" Tracy pleaded, torn.

"Maybe we ought to cut it right now," Brian said. "Just say goodbye. Before we start to tear each other up."

"I can't talk now, Brian—" Tracy begged.

"It's simple enough," Brian said, "before we get too invested in each other. Hey—"

"What?" Tracy said, so distracted by Sean's insistence that she barely heard him.

"Goodbye, Tracy," Brian said in a very low voice. He turned and walked away.

"Traaaacy!" Sean wailed.

"Will you, for Christ's sake, shut up!" she shrieked at him. And she was astonished to see him break into laughter, all the while taking pictures of her, her expression anguished, her hands on her hips, and her passionate dream making vulgar little noises as it gurgled down the drain.

"Terrific, Tracy," Sean called out, taking his camera away from his eye. "You never looked better." Then he ignored her and began ordering his assistants to mount the next setup.

Four

Later that night Tracy and Sean were standing outside Sean's hotel watching Giulio, Sean's young Italian assistant, load baggage and camera gear into the back of a taxicab. Tracy was numb with weariness and a sense of profound despair. This entire day had been shadowed with leave-takings–Brian's, and now Sean's. And it would be a long time before those shadows would lift. They would, she knew, get darker before they got brighter.

Sean teased her about her tragic expression. "You look so down," he said. "It's nice to see you're going to miss me but you don't have to get suicidal."

She said nothing.

He laughed and put his arm around her. "Oh, I know you're all cut up because your man walked out on you. But face it, you'd have been saying goodbye to him pretty soon anyway. It won't be more than a couple of weeks before you'll be in Rome. Let's see–I get to New York at midnight, check in to my hotel, drop the film around for processing first thing in the morning. Meet with my agent and a few editors tomorrow for lunch. I'll be on a six o'clock flight to Rome tomorrow night."

"I'm not going to Rome," Tracy said dully, "and let's cut out that jive. You know it is and I know it is. You've had some fun, I tried to help, and that's the end of it."

"Tracy." Sean turned her around by her shoulders so that he could command her full gaze. "There's something you'd better learn about me right now. I never make extravagant statements. Repeat: never. I never make promises I don't intend to keep. And there's one more thing. I don't *need* anything or anyone because I've got it all. So when I *want* something, I'm very careful about what I want and who I want–and I get it. I say you're coming to Rome. All you have to do is believe it."

"OK," Tracy mumbled, shrugging her shoulders. It was clear from her expression that she didn't care if she went to Rome or Fairbanks, Alaska. Sean understood her gloom and also understood that in due time she'd be desperate to leave this gloom behind her.

"You'll be hearing from me," he said as he got into the cab. She waved a hand limply as he drove off.

That night was one of the most difficult in Tracy's memory. She sat for long hours, hunched in a comfortable chair, her knees drawn up inside a ratty old flannel nightgown, a sodden handkerchief balled in her fist. A dozen times–a hundred times?–she started when she heard an imaginary noise in the hall. And just as many times she cursed herself for hoping that it was Brian. Now, at two thirty in the morning, she was so drained of emotion that she could barely feel anything anymore. But one thing was plain: she had to get on with her life. And getting on with her life meant getting out of her situation, out of this neighborhood, out of Chicago itself. In short, she'd better get on the track again.

Consequently, next morning, dressed as subtly and as cleverly as she knew how, carrying a portfolio of her latest sketches, she made the rounds of the garment center. She'd been over most of this territory, some of it more than once, but each time she returned to the attack she managed to single out a few places where she'd never been.

Now, sitting before a white designer in a high-priced dress house, she tried to contain her irritation as the man alternately plied his needle to a hem and, with a wet fingertip, flipped the pages of her portfolio.

"I'll tell you, doll," he drawled an epicene drawl, "a lot of this material isn't bad, really not bad at all. I mean it isn't as if you were just copying everybody."

"I've got others too," Tracy said. "This is just a fragment of my work."

He sighed and pushed up a heavy slave bracelet that was interfering with his needlework. "The trouble is," he said, "this is Chicago. Now you know you're good and I know you're good, but you're on the wrong curve, love. Good isn't what's being bought. So you just learn to get your kicks in other ways. I'm assuming you're straight."

"You're assuming," Tracy said.

"Hmm," he said, looking her over carefully, "because if you'd like to get into a different kind of scene, I could introduce you to some of *my* friends and the connections could do you a lot of good. Really."

Tracy was about to say something particularly savage but she bit her lip instead. She'd been here before, heard it before. Calmly she picked up her portfolio, gave him an elaborate wink, and sashayed out the door. Neither she nor the designer realized at that moment that she'd left one of her notebooks beside her chair.

Out in the street once more, she felt an overpowering desire to go back home—not to work—home. She wanted to pull the covers over her head and go to sleep. But that very fatigue, she knew, was the sign of cut-and-run. And she'd be damned if she'd do that. Instead, straightening her shoulders, she entered another building and went upstairs.

There the scene was shorter but more familiar than the preceding one. This time the manufacturer himself, a short, fat, energetic man, leafed quickly through her portfolio, allowing himself just enough time so that he wouldn't have to relight his smouldering cigar.

"Great stuff, kid," he said, "you got a nice little eye there. A nice little eye. But two things: first the line is all made up and we don't need any new ideas for this season, right? And second, we got a little girl who copies out stuff from the magazines and does a little presto chango and that's it. Now, let me tell you what I'm gonna do for you. It so happens, my secretary just quit. So if you can type a decent letter—"

"Oh, stuff it, will you?" Tracy said.

"What!"

"Jam it!"

"How do you like that! Out of the goodness of my heart—"

Tracy didn't hear the rest of it. She was out the door.

Deliberately, as if she were mortifying her flesh or doing a penitential *via crucis*, Tracy knocked on several more doors before deciding to call it a morning and go back to the office. She was tired, hungry, cross, and she was somewhat taken aback when Linda Evans met her with a sympathetic smile.

"What did the doctor have to say?" she asked Tracy sweetly. For a moment Tracy stared at her uncomprehendingly, then remembered just in time that she had called in early and left a message that she had a doctor's appointment that morning.

"Oh," she said, attempting to be offhand, "he said everything was in good shape. It was just a checkup, but you know how long it takes to get an appointment . . ."

"Oh, that's fine," Linda Evans said. "Your doctor gave you a clean bill of health?"

"Yeah," Tracy said, "said I might put on a couple of pounds, but other than that I'm as strong as a horse."

"That's good to know," Linda said, "because you're going to need your strength, dear. Looking for another job."

"What!"

"Your uh, *doctor* called about fifteen minutes ago and said you left a sketchbook in his consulting room."

Tracy sighed a rock-bottom kind of sigh.

After a few days of enjoying her leisure, manicuring her toenails, and sleeping as late as she wanted every morning, Tracy rose from her torpor and began pulling herself together again. Aside from the loss of money, which was critical, she didn't feel too badly about leaving the display department of Marshall Field. It was a dead end anyway, and the best you could say for it was that you could use it as a reference for another job. But what kind of job! That was the question. How did you go about getting a designing job when you had no professional credits? Well, she decided, that's what she would nevertheless try to do. But the first crucial step in that direction would be to sign up for unemployment insurance. She was in for a long siege.

Down at the unemployment bureau Tracy, all dressed up in a chic outfit chosen deliberately to offset the gloomy atmosphere of the place, moved patiently from one long line to the next. Oddly, unaccountably, her spirits began to rise. The lines were full of people, many of them obviously parents of small children, and most of them with a kind of wacky, what-the-hell attitude. It was clear that this wasn't the sort of place where people licked their wounds in public. The atmosphere was that of cheerful survivors of a shipwreck. Looking around her at the black and white faces of her fellow job hunters and chatting with people standing on long lines, she began to feel that life was worth living after all.

And as she stood in line she overheard a snatch of

conversation behind her. One young man leaned out of line and spoke to a friend in the opposite line. "Hey, brother," he called, "where'd you get that thing you're wearing?"

Tracy looked and saw another young man in the line parallel to hers, "Cat back there at the doorway," he said, "he's giving them away." Tracy took a look and saw that the fellow was wearing a large red-white-and-blue button with the words "BRIAN WALKER FOR ALDERMAN."

Craning her neck to see across the room, Tracy made out a knot of people near the doorway and she could see that Brian and Wil and some volunteers were handing out buttons as people moved past them. Brian, she could see, was in his element, greeting people, pressing the flesh, enjoying this grass-roots contact–the meat and potatoes of politics.

Slipping through the crowd, she made her way to another line of applicants not far from where Brian and his colleagues had set up their pitch.

"Hi, there," Brian said, "I'm Brian Walker. I'd sure like your vote for alderman."

"Are you an alderman?" the man asked.

"Not yet I'm not," Brian said, "but if enough people like you get behind me, I might have a pretty good chance."

"OK, man," the man said, "tell you what–you get me a job so I don't have to stand on these long lines here and I promise I'll vote for you."

"I can't promise a job but I can promise I'll give it my best shot," Brian answered amiably. "What's your gig?"

"Forklift operator, only I ain't had no work for the last three months. Case you didn't notice, there's what they call a recession goin' down. A recession is when you doin' all right, but a lot of *other* people ain't got jobs. Me, I'm one of those others."

"Let me think a minute." Brian frowned. "Hey, I know–Swifty Hannon, down at the I.C. warehouse. You know him? Seems like just yesterday I was talking to him and he's looking for people. Hey, Wil–give this man Swifty's phone number, will you?"

The appearance of immediate action brought a murmur of approval from the onlookers. A second man was encouraged to ask, "You know anybody looking for a turret lathe operator?"

"No," Brian said thoughtfully, "can't say as I do, but if you give your name to one of my people–and wear one of these buttons–" he grinned, "we'll see what we can do for you." As he pinned a button on the man's jacket, a woman's voice called out:

"Hey, Mr. Politician! I'm a widow from the West Side!"

"I hear you, sister," Brian said, looking around but not being able to find the owner of the voice.

Tracy had tucked herself in behind a couple of tall men and winked at her neighbors to let them know she was putting Brian on.

"My old man left me with six kids!" she shouted. "The heat's been turned off all this week and the kids is down with the flu. Now what are you gonna do about that?"

"Well, uh," Brian said, still unable to find the woman who spoke so boldly, "have you spoken–have you protested to your landlord, ma'am?"

"Landlord!" Tracy snorted, "I don't want no damn landlord. I want you to get my old man back!"

This brought a bellow of good-natured laughter and comments from the crowd. Brian knew he was being put on but didn't appear to mind. He took another look around and finally spotted Tracy. He broke into a broad grin and chose to play the game.

"The fact is, madam, that a foxy little lady like yourself shouldn't have no real trouble gettin' your old man back–unless of course, you turned off the heat on *him!*" This brought a big laugh. Brian had turned the tables. "Or was it," he resumed, "that you cut off his water?"

"Hell, I didn't cut nothin' off," Tracy shouted. "He just cut out is all."

"Madam, let me ask you," Brian said, "have you spoken to your block association?"

"Block association!" Tracy said woodenly, giving him a cue.

"Or don't you even have a block association?" Brian said.

"That's right," Tracy said, nodding to her neighbors and getting their answering nods. "We ain't got no 'sociation where I live."

"That's what I was afraid of," Brian said, frowning and shaking his head. "Now let me tell you, madam, and all of you folks–as the alderman of this district, my first act will be to organize block associations in every single neighborhood where they don't already exist. And once we get those associations going, you *use* them to make your needs known so that the City Council can do something about it. Unless you get your voice heard, nobody's gonna do anything for you. What I'm saying is, I will help you to help yourselves!"

This brought a round of applause.

"That's OK for you to say," Tracy called out, "but that still don't get my old man back."

"Well, madam," Brian said, "if you just step outside the door and wait for me, I'll see if I can't handle that little problem for you."

Tracy giggled and slid out the door, watching Brian hand out the last of his campaign buttons. She was jobless and broke and hadn't even got her first unemployment check but there was a fairly good possibility that she'd have her old man back.

Much later that night after they'd made love and now lay in bed talking, Brian said, "You know, while you're between jobs I could give you a little work. I mean I've got some union backing now and that gives me a little money for staff work. It wouldn't be much but it beats nothing at all. And you would be helping me. If you want to, that is."

"Don't talk silly, you know I want to help," Tracy said, "only I don't know the first thing about politics.

All I know is fashion. And not too damn much about that," she sighed.

"You could learn. Besides, mostly what I need is telephone answering, making calls, licking envelopes, that kind of stuff. I mean it's about the most undignified work in the world, but it helps to win elections. What do you think?"

"I think," Tracy said, "that since you helped to get my old man back for me, I ought to show you how grateful I am."

"You mean by licking envelopes!" Brian said slyly.

"No" Tracy said sensuously, "that wasn't the only thing I had in mind."

Over the next few weeks Tracy moved into a new world and, incidentally, to a new plateau of happiness. Work at Brian's headquarters was grubby, hilarious, hectic, one-half inspiration, the other half insanity. But somehow, falling over themselves, drinking cold coffee, running out of stamps, paper clips, wrestling with borrowed typewriters and herniated mimeograph machines, chipping in for hamburgers, and stamping their feet to keep warm in an underheated office—somehow they grew into a political action team.

Brian was, of course, at the center of all this activity, seemingly without nerves and without fatigue. He could be on his feet all day, barreling around the neighborhood in the VW bus, making speeches here, inspecting facilities there, stopping in at supermarkets to shake people's hands, passing out buttons to commuters, haranguing workers as they came out of factories, attending rallies at night and staying on until the early morning hours, writing a speech or going over the accounts. It seemed that the more he worked the more he thrived. He was truly, Tracy realized, a political animal. Most of all, he was exactly where he wanted to be, doing what he most wanted in life to do. No wonder, she thought, that he was never tired.

Tracy, on the other hand, although she didn't share Brian's incredible stamina, was so buoyed up by working with these dedicated volunteers and so stimulated by Brian's own enthusiasm that she almost forgot about her former life as she threw herself into the campaign. Her hours were almost as long as his. She ate when he ate, which was only some of the time, and slept when he slept, which was nearly never. And they went home at night to her house or to his house, scarcely knowing or caring which one it was. In fact, their clothes and other belongings were so scattered by this time that they'd almost lost track of where they'd left what.

The important thing was, no matter how exhausted they were and how many battles they'd lost during the day, when they fell into bed late at night there was always time for tenderness. And time for love.

One night when they had managed to get away from campaign headquarters early—about nine thirty—they were settled down in Tracy's pad. Tracy kneeled on the floor sketching out a new campaign poster, listening to the stereo playing softly in the background. Brian lay on the couch drafting a new speech on a legal pad. "Hey, honey, listen to this," he called out. "Give me a reaction."

He read: "Looking out for only number one, brings on separation, *dis*integration. What we've got to do is pull together, join our strength. The task is too big for individuals—try it separately and it will break you. But together, working jointly, I promise you, we can and will overcome." He glanced at her face and said quickly, "Of course it's a little cornball, but you've got to be emotional or you don't grab 'em. It's for a PTA luncheon. What do you think?"

Tracy shrugged. "Emotion! For a women's luncheon! You ask me, I'd say that's about as emotional as a box of graham crackers. Look, Brian, what have you got at the PTA? Women, right? So talk to them like women. 'You need more self-expression. Being a woman is more than just having babies. And getting with politics is just like having good sex—if you do it by yourself it not only ain't no fun, it don't do you no good.' Then you give 'em that big boyish grin of yours and that sexy laugh you've got. And that's it."

He laughed and dropped down beside her. "I knew you'd take to it. See? Already you're beginning to talk dirty, just like a politician. Hey, you wanna meet a congressman tomorrow night? I'm supposed to have dinner with this guy and I need his support. Why don't you come along?"

"Me? What have I got to say to a congressman?"

"Honey," Brian said, camping it up, "you don't got to say nothin'. All you got to do is flash that little girl grin of yours and bat those big brown eyes and let his mind do the rest."

"OK, OK," she laughed. "I get the message. Oh! Brian, I forgot. Tomorrow's Wednesday, right?"

"Usually follows Tuesday, except in leap year which is twenty-nine–"

"I mean, that's my design class!" Tracy said. "I can't miss that."

"Design class! Oh, come on, Tracy–this cat's a congressman, a party regular, he *expects* me to be there."

"OK, so go without me. I mean, all kidding aside, business is business, right? You don't need a chick with you to help you handle business."

"No," Brian insisted, "you don't understand. It's business, sure, but it has to *look* social. His wife will be there, and the city attorney and his wife–"

"But I'm not exactly your wife, am I?" Tracy said.

"That isn't important," Brian said, "what is important is that you be there with me–my woman. It's difficult to explain all the ins and outs of this kind of thing, Tracy, you have to play it by feel. And I really would like you there."

"No design class?"

"It's a matter of priorities, honey," Brian said.

"Whose priorities?" Tracy said. And then hastily, to cover the edge in her voice, she added, "OK, OK, I'll be there."

The dinner came and went. And for all that Tracy

spoke or for all that any of the men spoke to her she might, she thought, not even have been there. She regretted the fact that she'd given up her design class for such a useless exercise. Moreover, there was to be a design class show the following week and she needed to get last-minute instructions on that. It was only when they were all saying cordial good-nights in the foyer of the restaurant and the congressman pressed her hand with some unnecessary warmth that Tracy realized she might indeed have helped Brian. Still, a part of her resented the role and felt cheapened by it. Politics could be pretty ugly, she decided.

The following night she was in campaign headquarters late in the day and the joint was jumping. Tracy was trying to handle two phones at the same time and take notes on each call as well as make intelligent responses. No sooner did she hang up one phone when the other began to ring.

"Louise," she called plaintively to another volunteer, "I can't answer any more phones. I've got to get out of here."

Sweeping up her purse and her coat, she went over to Wil, who was stapling leaflets together. "Wil," she said, "the printer was out but promises to call back when he comes in—so you'll have to stand by for that."

Brian entered as Tracy backed toward the door. He gave her a quick hug.

"Hello," Tracy said. "Goodbye," as she moved toward the door.

"Hey, come back here," Brian called, moving toward his desk and reaching for a phone which seemed to spring into life when it saw him coming.

"I can't, Brian," Tracy called. "I have to go see Florence and pick up my dress from her. And then I've got to get my portfolio and go downtown."

"Yeah, yeah," Brian mumbled, not paying much attention to her. Then he cupped the mouthpiece of the phone and called to Tracy, "OK, see you at seven sharp. We've got to drive all the way to the other side of town."

"Drive! Where?"

"You remember, Tracy–the dinner. Independent Democrats. Hell, you set it up for me on the phone."

"Ohh," Tracy groaned. "I forgot. Anyway, I can't, Brian. I've got stuff I've got to do."

"Tracy!" Brian bellowed. "This is important. I need these guys' support!"

"Important for you! I'm trying to get ready for a design show next Thursday."

"But that's a whole week away," Brian protested.

"Maybe it is, but every big designer in town is gonna be there. It's where they get their apprentices. Which is how you break into this business at the professional level. And I really want to look good, Brian!"

"Damn it, Tracy, you've tried that. There isn't a one of those monkeys you haven't gone and interviewed. And they've all turned you down!" His voice faded when he saw the expression on Tracy's face. Brian realized that his impatience had brought him to the edge of a crude mistake.

"Look, honey." He attempted to ease her. "I just meant that it might be better not to get too much invested in–"

"Well, thank you, Brian Walker!" Tracy said in ringing tones, "for all that fine political support. And don't hold your breath while you're waiting for my vote!"

"Goddamn it, Tracy," Brian snapped, "you're behaving like a child. This dinner is important. It's a political reality and you're treating it–"

"I'm *not* treating it," Tracy said sharply, "I'm ignoring it, is what I am."

"What you are," Brian said, his temper escaping him, "is a pain in the ass, if you want to know the truth! You've got a chance to be involved in something meaningful here and you're blowing it all to hell."

"Meaningful!" Tracy shrilled. "*Your* career, you mean! *Your* ambition. *Your* election. What's so damned meaningful about that? What about *my* career, *my* ambition!"

"Your career doesn't exist, baby! It's all in your

head. Don't you think it's about time you came down to earth. Reality time, Tracy. You've been knocking yourself out, you've given it your best shot. Now forget it. It may be cruel but it's reality. And it's a hell of a lot less cruel than wasting your whole life on a dream that won't come true."

Tracy opened her mouth to reply and then closed it. She looked at Brian for a long time, speechless. Then, in a quiet voice, she said, "Fuck you, Brian," and walked out the door.

Walking numbly through the darkening streets, not even aware of the chill raw wind off the lake, Tracy traced the route back to her apartment. She let herself in, paused inside the door, and then, moving like an automaton, still wearing her coat and hat, she walked over to her drawing table. She began pulling sketches out of folders and stacking them in one pile. It was a mechanical act. She wasn't capable of really examining the sketches, wasn't sure whether she really wanted them or not, wasn't even really sure what she was going to do. A part of her mind told her that, as angry as she was at Brian, he had spoken nothing less than the truth. It *was* crazy to go on pretending that there was a future for her in fashion design. There wasn't any career, it was all hopes and dreams and tattered hopes and dreams at that. A part of her wanted to cleave to him, feel herself embraced by his strong protective arms so that she could cry like a little girl. And another part of her was desperately angry, urging action, flight, anything. In her confusion, she overturned a glass of water in which she'd been soaking some paintbrushes and she stooped to mop the water up off the rug.

At that point the telephone rang. She picked it up and for long seconds there were little clicks and burps and fragments of voices in a language she didn't understand. She wondered if she was going out of her mind.

Then a voice came through all that electronic chaos and she heard someone say, "Signorina Tracy Chambairs? *Allo? Allo?*"

"Yes," Tracy said impatiently, "who is it?"

"*Allo, allo?* Signorina Chamb-airs?"

"Stop clowning around," Tracy snapped, "I'm busy—"

Then she heard a businesslike voice. "This is the overseas operator. Rome calling for Miss Tracy Chambers. Is she there, please?"

"Yes—" Tracy gasped.

A moment later she heard Sean's voice. "Tracy, darling—" It sounded as if he were calling from the drugstore on the corner.

"It'll all set," Sean explained when Tracy had got over the shock of receiving a telephone call from halfway around the world. "They're waiting for you here. Dying to have you. I really gave it to them with those pictures I made of you back in Chicago. Now, I've checked the schedules. You can get a Chicago-Paris flight, that's nonstop, leaving in one hour from now. The airline has your ticket ready and they'll also have some cash for you when you identify yourself at the flight desk. When you get to Paris you will find a ticket waiting for you to Rome. And in Rome you'll find me. OK? Tracy? Did you get all that? Tracy?"

"Yes, yes," she said dimly, "I'm here. I—Sean. Is it really you? I mean, this couldn't be some crazy kind of gag—"

"Tracy, if you don't get on that plane," Sean said, "I am going to fly back there tomorrow morning and I'm going to get a piece of lead pipe and break every bone in your body. Do you hear me?"

"Yes, I hear you."

"Then you'll be on that plane?"

"I guess I haven't any other choice," Tracy said weakly.

"That's right, darling, you haven't. *A domani. A rivederci, cara. Ciao.*"

"What!"

"I said goodbye."

"Oh!" Tracy said. And a moment later, hung up the phone.

Exactly one half hour later, a numb Tracy, with two

suitcases packed, told her taxi to stop in front of campaign headquarters. The room was oddly quiet, except for Wil working in one corner. He looked up as she approached. "Hey," he said, "Brian really wanted me to tell you he apologizes, you hear? I mean, his nerves are getting a little snappish. Happens to a man who's running as hard as he is. Anyway, you're to go over to the Ambassador Hotel, and he'll meet you–"

"I came to say goodbye," Tracy said.

"Well, OK, that's nice," Wil said, "but get your ass in gear, will you, honey, because that dinner starts in an hour–"

"I mean really. Goodbye."

"You're walking out on him! You can't do that, Tracy," Wil said. "I just explained how racked up a man gets in a campaign like this. He didn't really mean–"

"I'm going to Rome."

"You–"

"Rome," Tracy repeated. "So goodbye."

Wil stared at her for a moment and then finally decided she was serious. "You're really doing it, hunh? That photographer cat?"

"Yes," Tracy said. "Wil?"

"Yeah?"

She held out her arms and she hugged him. "Take care of him, will you," she whispered.

"Sure, honey," Wil said. "And take care of yourself too, will you?"

She nodded and then went out and got into the cab.

Five

From the time Tracy entered the doorway of the airplane to the time her feet touched the carpeted corridors of Rome's Ciampino Airport, Tracy felt that her life was a waking dream. She had never flown before, let alone on an international flight, and she was totally unprepared for this unfamiliar experience. What first impressed her was the opulence, the almost sinful indulgence of the amenities and services. With her lifetime of deprivation and a background of almost continuous disadvantage, she was awed by—well, the seat, for example. It not only fitted her body as if it had been designed for her alone, it also suited her whim. It was soft to the point of voluptuousness and she was no sooner located in that upholstered cocoon than she was supplied with pillows, blankets, mints, cigarettes, sleek and glossy reading materials, and a never-ending service of food and drink. Having dined exquisitely, she felt, and having taken a child's delight in artful little saltcellars (which she prudently tucked in her purse), tiny whiskey bottles (one of which also went in her purse), and all the other ingenious plastic accompaniments to an airline meal, she settled into her headphones, tuned in a concert of the Moody Blues, and felt as if she'd gone on vacation. If only, she thought, she could see Aunt Florence in the seat next to her, being pelted with these same luxuries, her joy would be complete.

As it was, the seat next to her was unoccupied, so that when the stewardess, a beautiful, slim-waisted Korean girl, removed the intervening armrest and encouraged her to stretch out on both seats, Tracy hoped the flight would go on forever. Altogether, the passage was so smooth and her insulation from the world was so total that she lost all sense of time and distance. She might have been over the ocean or in outer space. She was conscious of the change from day to night but only dimly conscious, as if these matters no longer concerned her. Once she experienced a moment of anxiety when she realized that she was utterly helpless to affect her fate, that she was at the mercy of this giant machine and its crew and that her own will was valueless. But as she gazed around her at the other passengers, some of who were outright neighborly, and noticed their serenity, their atmosphere of unconcern, she gave herself up again into the aircrew's hands.

Paris was a blur of escalators and fast marches and hasty exchanges with airline functionaries and only a vague awareness that she was in another country. She had scarcely time to visit an earthbound bathroom before she was mounting another escalator and found herself inside another huge four-engined womb. A sense of sluggish movement, a dramatic and slightly sickening thrust, and she was off again, pointed in the direction, she hoped, of Rome.

Which city she entered shortly after twilight. As she moved quickly through customs and passport control and even, miraculously, found herself reunited with her pitifully shabby luggage (compared to the fat, rich cases of other travelers, her bags looked like underprivileged children), she began to appreciate how thoroughly Sean had organized her voyage. At every step she was anticipated by airline personnel who identified her quickly (Score one point for Black is Beautiful, Tracy thought) and led her through or around the administrative hurdles. There was even a handsome Italian who spoke excellent English waiting when she came through passport control to hand her into a waiting taxicab–though not before offering to take her into town in his own car if she could only wait around the airport for another hour until his shift ended. Tracy declined the offer pleasantly and was careful to close the door without slamming his fingers –they had, after all, only grazed, not grasped her.

Her first glimpse of Rome, as the taxi sped madly away from the airport and traveled the fabled Appian Way, was too much for her mind to take in. The blood-orange color of lowering sunlight on ancient walls and aqueducts was so overwhelmingly sensuous, her head actually throbbed with it. Wherever her eyes focused there was something that compelled her attention–a villa on a hillside, a flock of sheep, a fragment of marble statuary, an incredibly elegant gas station–and almost at once it was whisked away. She felt her eyes heavy with too much input, her brain seemed to be overstocked with images, each one falling upon the last so that she was dizzy with it all.

And when the cab raced through the gates of the city itself, she gave herself up to a feeling of dismay. She would never, she was certain, be able to take it all in. Watching a traffic cop direct auto flow like a ballet dancer caused her to spin around in her seat. And no sooner did her eyes fix on him than her attention was claimed by an enormous horse drawn hearse with glittering silver trappings and black ostrich feather plumes. Her gaze was snatched away by a devastating little sports car and then to a news kiosk bursting with colorful posters, and then to a glimpse of the Colosseum which took her breath away. The Colosseum! she marveled, not quite able to believe that she was actually passing the structure. Not able to believe that it was she, Tracy Chambers in this taxi, circling around that building which she had seen on posters and in picture books all her life. It wasn't a poster or a picture book. It was real. She was there! HERE! she corrected herself, with a gasp.

And then suddenly she found the taxi had stopped in a quiet urban street, narrow, cobblestoned, and old. What century? what period was this facade, that wall? She had no idea. It had a nice quiet neighborhood kind of feel and she was grateful to be in an environment that somewhat resembled—except for its cleanliness and excellent repair—her own, back home.

The taxi driver removed her bags and helped her out of the cab. He spoke no English but indicated by sign language that he would take enough money from the notes in her hand to pay the amount listed on the taximeter. As he meticulously helped himself, Tracy did a fast mental arithmetic, decided that a tip of 300 percent was overdoing things just a bit, grabbed back one of her banknotes and bade him a muttered "*Ciao*, Buster!"

A moment later, bags in hand, she rang the bell on a battered second-floor doorway and found herself face to face with a grinning Sean McAvoy who stood smiling and self-assured as ever, holding a fresh drink in his hand.

Reaching out, he drew her to him and kissed her. "I gave you one more hour," Sean said, "and if you hadn't shown up by then, I was coming after you."

"Don't expect me to say anything that makes sense," Tracy said, stepping inside his apartment, "my mind is so completely blown I may never get it together again."

"I'll put these in your bedroom," Sean said, "and then I'll show you around."

"Bedroom! You mean—"

"For tonight," Sean said. "It's kind of silly to go to a hotel when I've got a four-bedroom apartment. Tomorrow morning I'll show you the apartment I've picked out for you. Your own apartment. You'd like that, wouldn't you?"

"Uh, sure—of course, only—"

"How do you pay the rent?"

"Yeah, something like that," Tracy said.

"Don't worry about it. The first month's rent is paid. And unless I'm way off base, you'll be earning ten times as much as you'll be needing within another week. You can pay me back the first month's rent out of your earnings."

Tracy was too dazed to question him. She shrugged and smiled and then reacted with surprise to the room around her. He'd taken her into a narrow, high-ceiling room that was literally covered with photographs—some in black and white, some in color, some blown up to poster size, some merely tiny contact strips. They were on the walls and ceiling and even on the floor. There was hardly a square inch of surface in this room that was not covered with photographs. And they were all of the same woman—or parts of her. Her eyes, lips, bust, hair, full figure, profile, torso. She was one of the most beautiful women Tracy had ever seen, a tall, broad-shouldered blonde who looked like a Viking goddess.

"Oh, this," Sean said, slipping into his habitually ironic tone, and flicking a photo poster with his finger, "is my last duchess. Her Excellency, Lady Philomena Sharpes-Cooper dei Caravaggi. Not bad, eh?"

"Bad! I've seen her on every magazine cover on the newsstand for the last fourteen months. You mean, you've done all those."

"Uh-hunh," Sean said casually. "I've done her and been done by her. She's been on every magazine cover in the world and beneath every bedcover in Rome. In fact, she's the only woman I've ever known who was picketed by a group of local prostitutes—they walked up and down in front of her house saying she was unfair competition to local labor."

Tracy looked at him carefully, noting the traces of anger tugging at the corners of his mouth. "And you really got hung up on her?"

Sean shrugged. "I never get really hung up on anybody, Tracy. And that includes you too. What I do, I do for kicks. Get me?"

"Yeah," Tracy said, "I'll keep that in mind." And to herself, she thought, I wonder why he has to come on with that tough-guy pose, that little-boy-tough-guy pose.

"Look, Sean," she said, "you're talking to a ghetto chick, right? I mean, I'm just a po' chile. So explain to me how I'm gonna live, please? I mean, unless I can get the numbers in my head, unless I know I'm going to cut it and where and how—well, I get nervous. I can't sleep. Can you dig what I'm saying?"

"Sure," Sean smiled pleasantly, amiably again. "OK, for openers, you've already got some money coming to you for the ad I did."

"Ad? What—"

"The pics I shot of you in Chicago. I managed to place them. You'll get a few hundred from those. Oh, the apartment I've got for you is really a steal—a friend of mine is going back to New York for a year and all he wanted was someone reliable who'd sort of look after the place. For one-third the usual rent. I think it'll cost you about sixty a month. And tomorrow morning, after you've had a good night's sleep, I'm going to take you around to your first job assignment."

"First job assignment!"

"The agency. It's the top agency in Rome, the best in Europe. They'll fall all over you, don't worry. Now—undo that top button."

He had taken up a camera and was adjusting the shutter. "I could open every button," Tracy said, grinning, "and I couldn't stand alongside her—" she motioned to the superb breasts of the duchess.

"She's not a *her*," Sean said, starting to snap pictures as he moved in a restless circle around Tracy. "That's an *it*. A thing. I prefer to give inanimate names to all of my creations. She was known as Crystal. Something hard and cold. And sharp."

OK," Tracy said, laughing. "I got the perfect name for me: coat hanger. That's what I look like, isn't it? A black wire coat hanger?"

Sean continued snapping pictures, never taking his eye from the viewfinder as he talked. "No, there ought to be a term for something that is rich, darkly beautiful, with some hint of the exotic, something that suggests warmth and strength—I've got it! Mahogany. That's it. From now on you'll be introduced as Mahogany. Forget about Tracy Chambers, she is no more."

"Mahogany. Mahogany." Tracy said the word slowly, getting the feel of it on her tongue. "I don't know if I like that."

"You'll like it," Sean said, "because I like it. And from now on, whatever I like you'll like until, that is, you begin to acquire a sense of taste on your own. That'll be a while though, it'll take some doing."

"A sense of taste on my own! Are you for real! What the hell do you think I am, a windup doll? Who do you think designed the clothes you photographed, the dress I'm wearing? That's *me*, Tracy Chambers."

"Mahogany," he said calmly.

"*Tracy Chambers*," she said grimly.

"Mahogany," Sean said quietly. "Or fuck off!"

Tracy was startled. His face was white and quietly furious. She had never seen him this way before and yet she knew without any question that he would have his way or else.

He explained quietly as she stood there with her mouth open. "I'm running the show for now. There'll come a time when you'll spread your wings and want to fly—as the song says. Not yet. You follow me. I'm the papa bird and the mama bird and you'll stay in the nest—or get kicked out on your ass. Now, can you live with that?"

Tracy thought for long seconds. There was a part of her that urged her to pick up her suitcases and turn around and leave. She had no doubt that he would hold the door open for her, had no doubt also that he would see to it that her airline ticket was paid for and all arrangements laid on. She didn't like his arrogance and there was something else that was worse—some hint of savagery, perhaps even madness, that lay underneath.

On the other hand, he was insisting on a kind of apprenticeship that was no more than fair—and sensible. What the hell did she, Tracy Chambers, know about haute couture, about the world of international fashion, about modeling for that matter, about Rome—about anything, really? What the hell did she know? And was she such a little idiot that she would throw away her one chance to learn! Was *she* so arrogant in fact, that she couldn't take a little discipline and a little rough treatment from a pro, or did she have to run back home to mama? *What* mama? she thought:

"I understand that you'll be calling the shots, Sean," Tracy said, "and I accept that. But don't expect me to take every decision without opening up my mouth. I accept that you'll be running things, but you've gotta give me the freedom to raise an occasional squawk."

"Sure," he smiled, "squawk your head off," he said, "just so long as we're agreed on the rules."

"OK, teach," Tracy said with tired good humor, "so what's the first step."

"The first step," Sean said, putting his camera down at last, "is that I take you over to the agency and you charm their asses off."

"Whose asses, what agency?"

"Gavina. *The* agency. I've already got them halfway committed, that is, one of the head faggots, a guy by the name of Giuseppe, is all steamed up about you. He's the one who bought the pictures I made in Chicago. But he's only a front man. They need me, so I've got a lot of leverage. But I've still got to get you OK'd by the brass. What I'm going to do is run a small layout of you wearing Princess Galitzine originals. The princess is a friend of mine and is doing me a favor by letting me have some advance stuff out of her latest collection. I figure the combination of those threads and your talent ought to do the trick."

"Why do I have to wear somebody else's clothes, Sean? I've got my own designs. Can't I model those? I told you where I want to be and modeling doesn't do it for me. I don't mind it as a temporary thing–"

"Tracy," Sean said gently, "don't try my patience, please. I'm calling the shots. You're nothing until you've got some power in this business. And that's going to take a little buildup. Once you get power you can use it. So let's just take it one step at a time. Now, I want you to take your clothes off and rub your body with oil while I set these lights up. I'm going to do a bunch of nude shots of you just to perk up your portfolio."

"Nude shots! Aren't most of these guys gay?"

"They're not all guys, darling. Some of them are women. And you're right–they're gay. So get undressed, will you?"

"But it's late and I'm getting tired."

Sean exploded. "What the hell do you think this is, a goddamned picnic! You want to get somewhere, don't you? Well you don't make it at the top unless you work your ass off. Now, GET WITH IT. NOW!"

I feel like I've been drafted, Tracy said to herself as she began to unzip her dress. Like I'm in the army now. Thank God, she thought, they can't send me to Vietnam.

The following day Tracy rose at ten thirty to find the sun streaming through her bedroom window. Opening the shutters, she looked out at a glorious view of Roman rooftops, and when she drew back into the room, saw that Sean had already deposited an attractive breakfast tray. She drank the delicious *caffè-latte* that he had prepared, and luxuriously showered. Her spirits rose and she was beginning to feel deliciously pampered when the intercom crackled. Sean's voice, exasperated, nervous, filled the room. "OK," he snapped, "you've been taking your damn good time, how about you get down to the studio on the double. Some of those shots I made last night are lousy and I want to do some retakes. I'm still in the darkroom but just go down there and wait for me."

Tracy sighed and did as she was told. For an hour they worked in silence except for Sean's brief, staccato commands. His intensity was something awesome, she realized, and he seemed to withdraw entirely into his camera. She found that she was beginning to respond to his commands with a similar kind of concentration so that, although they were separated, there was a kind of bond between them.

As soon as this shooting session was finished, Sean said, "I want to put these in the darkroom, then you've got to get your hair done–"

"But, I–"

"Get your hair done," he repeated, "then lunch, then a nap, then get dressed–don't think about it, I'll tell you what to wear. And then at five o'clock we're due at the agency."

"At five o'clock! Aren't people going home from the office at that hour?"

"Not in Rome, dear. Five o'clock is when everything happens. Half the business in Rome is done between five and five thirty. The rest doesn't get done."

The elegant interior of the Gavina agency was more than a little awesome. An absolutely stunning girl sat alone at an enormous rough marble table in the center of a gleaming rosewood floor. A single baby spotlight turned her auburn hair into a long sheet of flame. There was nothing else in this vast reception area, nothing and no one. Not even, Tracy noticed, a telephone.

Sean approached the desk and the girl raised heavy-lidded eyes, gleaming with black and turquoise makeup, giving him a questioning look. "Just tell Signor Gambarelli I'm here," Sean said quietly.

This gorgeous creature languidly pressed a hidden button on the edge of the great slab of marble and spoke briefly. "*Il fotografo americano, con una ragazza nera, vi aspettano.*"

There was a small chiming sound and then a section of ancient brick wall pivoted to reveal a doorway. Thrilled with all of this drama, Tracy whispered to Sean as they entered the inner offices, "Who was that gorgeous girl? Is she a model too?"

"He," Sean answered with a wry smile. "That's a transvestite. One of Giuseppe's favorite flavors–strawberry."

Tracy shut her mouth with a snap.

Signor Giuseppe came out of his office to greet them, a plump, effusive little man who gave off an atmosphere of enthusiasm and a heavily floral cologne. "*Ah, che bella fanciulla*," he intoned, smiling at Tracy, kissing her hand, and dancing around her like an excitable sparrow.

"Have you got everybody lined up inside?" Sean asked briefly.

"But of course, *caro*," Giuseppe said, "you know me, Sean-ino, when I do a 'ype–you call it 'ype, no?" he said to Tracy. She couldn't help laughing at this strange blend of hip and Italian-accented English.

"That's what you call it," she agreed.

"Ah, you see, I am right on, no," Giuseppe said, proud of his vernacular, and taking Sean's arm. "All you have said about Signorina Chamb-airs, I agree two thousand percent."

"Mahogany," Sean said.

"*Scusi*–" Giuseppe looked blank.

"Mahogany. From now on. That's the product label. It's my product and don't you forget it. Not Gavina's product, mine. You people don't want to buy in, I've got two tickets booked for Paris tonight. We'll be talking to Magnum and Givenchy and that whole crowd in the morning."

"Ah, but that is impossible, Sean–you promised," Giuseppe protested, "and after all my 'ow you call? spadework. That's not fair."

"Yeah, well, here's your spade and she's ready to work, so let's get with it," Sean snapped.

Giuseppe's face hardened and Tracy suddenly saw

that there was more to this man than plump pleasantries. You didn't stay alive at the top in this business by being a butterball.

They paused before two huge polished doors which were austerely marked with a single word: Gavina. Tracy quailed. It was plain that she was to go through those doors–alone.

Sean pulled her to one side. "OK," he muttered, "Giuseppe will take you in and introduce you–and that's it. From then on you're on your own. Don't worry, they've been prepped, they're expecting you. They'll look you over like a piece of meat on a butcher's hook but it won't kill you. Keep cool and hang tough. Do you understand me? Hang tough. These people aren't just looking at your ass, they want to know if you've got the guts inside to make it. OK, go!"

He gave her a little shove toward Giuseppe. That man opened the door, motioned for her to preceed him, and Tracy found herself in a large no-nonsense sort of conference room. Along one side of the conference room was a long severe table and seated at that table, almost as if they were a panel of judges, were five men and one woman in the center. Their faces were absolutely neutral as Tracy walked in.

"*Signora e signori,*" Giuseppe said effusively. "*eccola qui, la signorina che si chiama Mahogany, la ragazza di Signor McAvoy!*"

There were faint smiles of greeting and murmured remarks followed by a devastating silence. Tracy smiled briefly and then remembered Sean's hissed instructions, "Hang tough." She assumed her most haughty manner.

"Would you please remove that–uh–jacket you are wearing, signorina?" one elegant and strained-looking man said. She took off the jacket and let it fall on the table in front of him.

"And would you turn around, please?"

Tracy turned.

"Once more, please–and slowly. Very slowly."

Tracy did an exaggeratedly slow pirouette.

"Hmm," the man said.

"Do you smile, signorina?" another man asked. "Surely, there are times in your life when you must smile."

Obligingly, Tracy managed a smile, astonished that she could fake it.

"*Divina*," another man intoned, "a superb smile."

"Yes, I agree, Roberto," said yet another man, "but we are not selling dental cream, after all. We're in the fashion business, am I correct? And this young woman has the bosom of a young child—forgive me, signorina."

"A matter of no importance," one man said. "In a few weeks, with a silicone implant we can give her a bosom like Sophia Loren."

"Pardon me"—the rejoinder was acid—"Sophia Loren we don't want. We're selling perfume, no? We want beautiful breasts, not enormous—but at least something. This is nothing"

"Please, please," another man said, "let's not argue about silicone—what about the legs? Slim, no? Very fashionable. But the thighs? Will you pull up your dress, signorina, and show us your thighs?"

Tracy did as she was told. She was feeling cold now, utterly cold, as if she had turned to metal inside. At first the shock of being discussed like a side of beef caused her so much pain that she wanted to run. But Sean's warning somehow gave her strength. "Hang tough?" That she would, by God!

"Nice thighs. Very sexy, very shapely. Those we can use, without question."

"The thighs I agree, but *scusi, Armando, il culo, non c'e mica niente!* The derriere, signorina, it is very small. I regret . . ."

"Oh, I do too," Tracy said acidly. "I do regret. I can always add a pound or two of silicone to my boobs, but that ass is a problem. Tell you what, I'll work on it, see if I can build it up real good. And when I get it blown up a little, I'll bring it around and you all can kiss it. Is that clear? So if you don't mind, I'll just run along now . . ." Tracy said, snatching her jacket up from the table.

"But, signorina!—" voices murmured protest.

"Listen," Tracy said sharply, "what you want is some kind of a living manniquin, OK? That's your business. But it ain't me. Use that girl you got there, your secretary. She's pretty, she's got good boobs. I can't see her ass from here but—she'll probably be able to handle it."

Tracy's hand was on the doorknob when the woman called out to her. "Signorina Mahogany—a moment, please." Tracy turned and saw that the woman had risen. Now that she was standing, Tracy saw that although she had a truly superb figure, she was a bit older than she had appeared. Older and somehow more authoritative.

"I'd love to be a model myself," the woman said, "but if I did that, then I should have to leave the running of the business to these idiots." She gestured at the men on either side of her.

Smiling, she added, "I am Compagnia Gavina. Carlotta," she said, extending her hand. Tracy took her hand uncertainly.

"Now, dear," Carlotta said, "tell me when it would be convenient for you to come to work."

A few minutes later Tracy found herself out on the sidewalk, staring blankly around her. She heard a voice and saw Sean calling to her from a nearby sidewalk café.

"Well," she said limply as she slid into a chair and he pushed a drink across the table, "I've got no tits and I've got no ass . . . Oh, my thighs are OK and the smile is pretty good if you wanna sell toothpaste . . . But," she said, "I guess I'm hired."

"That's good," he said briefly. "Now I'm going to have to defuse half a ton of plastic explosive that I stashed all over that joint."

"Plastic—what!" Tracy shrieked.

"You don't believe me? You think I wouldn't have blown the place up?"

Tracy broke into hysterical laughter. "I believe, I

believe," she said, waving her hands in the air like a gospel singer. The smart patrons in the café all turned to stare at her with grateful smiles. She even got, from one or two would-be gigolos, a spattering of applause.

"To the birth of Mahogany, kid." Sean grinned, raising his glass.

"The first day." Tracy smiled back, touching his hand. "The first day of the rest of my life!"

Six

For the first time in her life Tracy found herself at peace with her environment. The apartment that Sean had found for her in Trastevere (literally, "across the Tiber," or "the other side of the tracks") was so charming, so civilized—though not luxurious—that she discovered what it meant to live in a place designed by people and for people. It was a very far cry from the average Chicago tenement, which is at best a "housing device" and at worst a profit-making "dormitory." The scale of the rooms, the oddly shaped windows from which one got a never-ending variety of views, the sense of peace, all of this more than compensated for a small and not very good stove, a tiny balky refrigerator, and a water heater that worked only on its good days. Material comforts weren't all that important, Tracy learned, when your spirit was able to soar.

And soar she did from morning until very late at night.

Sean had made her into a star. She had scarcely been working in Rome a week when the first of Sean's photographs was splashed all over local billboards. There she was, elegant, grave, and totally absorbed while a waiter poured her glass full of a golden liqueur and the legend read: MAHOGANY'S DRINK? MANZONI, OF COURSE! Riding on the back of Sean's motorcycle at the time, crossing a Roman piazza that was like a modern gladiatorial combat, with bloodthirsty motorists hurtling across the square from all directions, Tracy whooped with surprise and almost fell off the bike.

"That's me!" she shrieked. "Up there–look!"

"What?" Sean shouted, doing his best to avoid tangling with a racing Ferrari.

"Up there–look! look!" She pounded him on his shoulders and they almost swerved into a truckload of artichokes on their way to market.

"Oh, that," Sean said offhandedly when he'd pulled his motorcycle up out of traffic. "Not bad, considering they had to reproduce it in such a hurry. I think they should have held back the red plate a little and given it a touch more yellow, but not bad."

"Red! Yellow!" Tracy shrieked. "What are you *talking* about. That's *me!* Me, nine feet tall. In the middle of Rome. Drinking that fancy booze. Hey, wait a minute, I don't remember posing for that."

"That's because you were stoned out of your mind, darling."

"Stoned! Never. I was not. You snuck that picture, didn't you? While I was having a drink at your apartment. You popped that thing and then gave it to the agency."

"That's right," he grinned. "It'll take you a while before you're totally unselfconscious while posing. It isn't something you can learn overnight. So for the time being I have to get some of my stuff while you're not paying attention."

"Sean—" Tracy hesitated. "Am I—will I be—you know—paid for that?"

"Sure," he said. "A hundred dollars for the shooting session—which is fair enough, considering that there wasn't any shooting session. Plus two hundred in rental fees from the agency and a royalty based on exposure and frequency. I'd say you'll net—oh, maybe a grand out of that shot."

Tracy was a long time before she could talk. "You mean," she said finally, "out of that one shot—while I was, as you say, stoned out of my mind."

"That's right," Sean said. "You want to know what your probable income will be over the next year—and that's just the beginning, the buildup?"

"I—I'm afraid to ask," Tracy said. "Like I don't want to tempt fate."

Sean grinned. "I'm almost afraid to tell you—and for the same reason. But I'll tell you this: by the end of the year you'll be middling rich, impossibly arrogant, and your closest friend will be your business manager."

It wasn't, of course, just a matter of having money for the first time in her life—enough money, more than enough, go-to-hell money. It was also the acceptance. First, her immediate neighbors in the building and in the street where she lived. They all recognized her as "Mahogany," and there were smiles and hugs wherever she went. The husband and wife who sold her fresh fruit from their wheeled cart asked her for an autograph and always slid an extra apple or orange into her shopping bag.

In the little neighborhood trattoria where she frequently took her meals she was greeted as if she were a member of the family, invited to eat with the owner's wife or his friends, introduced to all the regulars, and assured the best cut of the pork roast when that was the day's special. "Mahogany," she was the local celebrity, "*la ragazza americana delle riviste*," the American girl from the magazines. And she loved every moment of it.

A black girl in a sea of whites, she no longer felt

invisible the way she had felt in American white communities most of her life. People did not look past her, around her, through her—they greeted her with shouts and kisses, with winks and smiles. Acceptance. It was like bright red wine.

And not only in her neighborhood, which was working class mixed with petit bourgeoisie. She found acceptance also in fashion circles, which is to say, at the highest levels of Roman society. Most of the major fashion houses were literally top-heavy with aristocrats. There were contessas and marchesas and principessas by the dozen. Most of them were well educated, well traveled, and nearly all of them spoke good-to-flawless English. Among these people as well, Tracy —no longer Tracy, she had even begun to think of herself as Mahogany—was a darling, adopted, adored.

Finally, Sean McAvoy himself had begun to change his attitude toward her. It was no longer an inflexible master-slave, teacher-student relationship. More and more they approached collaboration. Sean, who was anything but stupid, quickly recognized that Mahogany's innate good taste made up for her lack of experience. So when she said "That doesn't feel right to me," or "Why don't we try it this way" he found himself beginning to listen, and in fact, to learn.

As for him, he had never worked with a model like Mahogany before. Most of the girls he had known, however beautiful, however talented, were either neurotic or stupid or both. There were endless problems, rages, tantrums, illnesses both real and imagined. Mahogany radiated a professional competence twenty-four hours a day. The more they worked and the harder they worked, the more she seemed to enjoy it. Late night sessions seemed only to inspire her and on half a dozen occasions Sean found himself incorporating her ideas into the shot. In fact, one night when he was totally bereft of ideas and was simply clicking his camera automatically to pile up prints, Mahogany dashed out of the studio, raced across the street to where her butcher was just rolling down his heavy steel awning for the night, and came back with a freshly skinned pink rabbit in her hand. That shot–Mahogany in a skintight white evening gown, staring at a pink rabbit with a look of faint distaste, made the cover of two European fashion magazines at the same time and was the talk of fashionable Rome.

A kind of rough-and-ready camaraderie sprang up between them. True, Sean was still boss of their enterprise, but Mahogany was very nearly his peer. One late afternoon after they had been working for hours around the fountains in the Piazza Navona and had bought ice cream for an endless supply of street urchins who gathered around in regiments, Sean mopped his brow and closed the legs of his tripod.

"Tired?" he said. "Rcady for a drink?"

"Tired!" she laughed, "us field hands don't get tired; it's you house niggers who're always feeling weak."

"I don't know," Sean said moodily, "maybe we ought to try something different–different location–indoors maybe."

"But there's all kinds of stuff in this piazza we can use, Sean. We've only just got started."

"You've got to be kidding," he said. "You mean you're not sick and tired of it?"

"No! I love it!"

"Hey, look," he said, coming close and adopting a confidential tone, "don't you think you could get just a little bit sick of it? So we can go home?"

"Shoot!" she said contemptuously. "You ofay dudes, you about to run outta genes, ain't you. I mean, talk about decadent!"

He shrugged and grinned, and then, while her mouth was open for laughter, bumped her over the low parapet of the fountain so that she landed on her butt in the pool.

As she came up laughing and shrieking, blowing water and wiping wet hair out of her eyes, Sean, doubled over with laughter, squeezed off a dozen or more shots.

Two weeks later there was Mahogany on a billboard, streaming water, spray coming off her hair, looking like some crazy sea witch who'd just emerged from the water. And huge letters proclaimed: MAHOGANY S'IMPAZZISCE PER FOSCHIA DEL MATTINO, and below her torso was a crystal bottle of perfume.

It seemed that, together, they could do no wrong.

And it was also true that Carlotta Gavina, whose agency was acquiring a new distinction as the home of the inimitable Mahogany, had become a close and good friend.

One evening, as they were walking down the street, just having finished a TV commercial, Carlotta couldn't contain her enthusiasm. "Divine," she said to Tracy. "We Italians overuse that word but there's no other." She gave the girl a warm hug and a kiss on the cheek.

"Oh," Tracy said, only half kidding, "it wasn't me at all. With the great Signor McAvoy behind the camera, even a dust mop takes on glamour."

"That's true," Carlotta said teasingly, "if he happens to be in love with that dust mop."

Sean gave her a deadly look.

"Well," Tracy said, ignoring the glances that passed between Sean and Carlotta, "I kinda think I like this divine bit. I'll have to admit it. I *am* just a little bit divine. Of course," she added, "I have Teach to thank for that. Sean taught me divinity."

"Ah, yes," Carlotta agreed, "he is one of the world's great teachers. Except," she paused, "he has an aversion to graduation day."

Tracy looked at Carlotta, sensing that she was no longer joking. And then she looked at Sean, but his expression was blank.

As they came abreast of a news kiosk, Carlotta bought a handful of glossy magazines and fanned them out for Tracy to see. *Harper's Bazaar*, *Vogue*, *Elle*, *Oggi*, *Du*, *Tempo*, and half a dozen more top European publications. Tracy's picture was on the cover or on the inside front or back cover of each one of them. "Sensational," Carlotta said. "You see now what the Gavina agency can do for you. I think we could place your picture in an Eskimo magazine if there was one."

"Well, don't pretend that you're doing it for love, love," Sean said acidly. "We're putting an awful lot of bread in those aristocratic pockets of yours."

And the very aristocratic Carlotta gave Sean a fixed look and said, "Don't get cute with me, Jack. I don't like that at all."

It was the first time Tracy had ever seen anyone bad-mouth Sean and get away with it. Carlotta, she thought, must have some kind of a lock.

Much later that night, after a long leisurely dinner on the Pincio, they sat in Sean's apartment sipping brandy and listening to old 78's from the forties. Tracy wore a typical next-to-nothing gown that she'd designed and was barefoot, stretched out on the thick carpet, her head cushioned on a fur-covered pillow. Sean sat next to her, brooding over his drink. With one lean finger, he traced an unquiet path up and down her bare arm. Tracy found the sensation disturbing, partly arousing and partly uncomfortable. She wasn't sure whether she wanted him to go on or to stop.

Lost in these speculations, she did not notice that Sean was fixing her with an intense stare.

"What do you see?" she finally asked him. "What is it you see that you haven't seen a thousand times in your viewfinder? Is there anything left? any aspect of me you don't already know?"

"What we see," he said briefly, "depends on what we want to see. Depends on how we look." He smiled but there was no humor in it.

"That's neat, but you haven't answered my question," Tracy insisted.

"Tracy Chambers," he said. "She's gone. I can hardly even remember her. What I see is Mahogany."

"You! You say that? I don't like you calling me Mahogany, Sean, not when we're like this. It puts distance between us. You're Sean. I'm Tracy. Nothing has changed. Not really."

"You're Mahogany," he said simply. "I made you."

"Oh–" she hesitated. "I'm not forgetting that. I know what I owe you, Sean. Everything. Simply everything. In that sense you're right–I'm yours."

"Are you? You really feel that?"

She was about to answer but he put a hand on her breast, pressing, urging, and she felt her nipple grow hard. Then he bent and kissed her. She lay still, feeling his mouth on hers and feeling also a kind of sadness. Because as much as she wanted to rise to him, as much as she wanted to reward him with the passion he deserved, the feeling simply wasn't there.

At length she pushed him gently away. "Sean," she said, fumbling for words, "this–it's not us, Sean. It just isn't our thing." He turned instantly away.

"Oh, Sean–have I hurt you? I don't want to, you must know that."

He was silent. She reached for his hand but he pulled it away.

"Sean, please–" She sat up now, alarmed, trying to turn his face so that she could look into his eyes. "The last thing I would ever want to do is hurt you. But this –it just isn't necessary, Sean. It isn't a gig we have to do. There's nothing we've got to–well, prove!"

"Prove!" Sean exploded. "Who says I'm trying to prove anything? Who? Carlotta? Did she fill you in on the psychology of Sean McAvoy, is that it?"

"Carlotta!" Tracy said. "Carlotta hasn't been talking to me–and anyway, even if she did? What's that got to do with us? I don't need Carlotta to tell me what kind of man you are, Sean."

"The point is, I am a man, Tracy!" Sean said.

"I know you are–"

But she was unable to continue. Sean embraced her in a passionate, wiry grip and there was no mistaking his urgency now. His hands were everywhere on her body, removing the thin wisp of a dress which barely covered her naked thighs, lifting her, pressing her to him. She felt his mouth warm on her flesh and felt her own responses beginning to awaken. Oh, please, she prayed silently, let me come alive, let me give him what he needs, what I know he needs.

She allowed Sean to lift her and carry her into the bedroom. There he laid her carefully on the bed and began to explore her body with his mouth and with his hands. There was something nervous, almost frantic about the way he touched her, the way his tongue moved over her flesh, and as she felt his warm breath on her thighs, she parted her legs gratefully, feeling the excitement begin to mount in her so that she brought herself up to meet him. She writhed against him as she felt his long supple fingers on her buttocks, felt his tongue flicking inside her body so that a rhythmic pulse began to move her. Her breath came more quickly and she found herself beginning to moan with pleasure, wanting him to stop toying, teasing. "Oh, please, Sean," she begged, "come inside me. Now. I want you. Come inside me."

But he ignored her, breathing heavily against the wetness of her body, biting her, seeking her, urging her with his mouth. "Please," she gasped, "please." And then she could wait no longer. She found all her need building to such a peak that she could only cry out helplessly and thrust herself against him until her strivings had subsided.

Moments later, she reached for him and found him limp, incapable. "Oh!" she sighed softly, reaching for him. "Let me." Angrily he pushed her hand away. "No," she insisted, bringing her head to his body, kissing his flat belly and moving down so that she could take him in her mouth. He lay there quietly, unmoving. And she tried to urge him into life, mouthing him, caressing him, molding him with her fingers, with her tongue—but it was no use. She felt a bitter sense of disappointment, almost of shame. It was as if she had cheated him, had taken what he had offered and been gratified by it, but had been unable to do anything for him in return. She was, she thought, she must be—a failure.

She rose to look at Sean and when she saw his

face she knew that the failure wasn't hers. His eyes were closed but his cheeks were wet. He had been crying.

Tenderly, maternally, she cradled his head against her breast and began to rock him. "Don't," she said. "Don't, Sean, you mustn't. It was wonderful for me. Couldn't you tell that? Wonderful."

He said nothing and she fell silent as well. For a long time she held him, and then covered him and put a pillow beneath his head. Sean lay with his head turned away from her, unwilling to let her see his face.

"Sean," she tried once more. "It doesn't matter. Don't you see that? We're beyond that. It doesn't matter."

But it did matter—to him. She could see that, could feel it. And there was nothing she could do to help. And there was nothing, she realized, that she could do to ease his pain.

A week or so later she discovered just how deeply he was hurt. And she also understood that, although she was not responsible for his hurt and indeed, had done everything possible to avoid it and ease it—he would never forget or forgive.

They were shooting a TV commercial on the outskirts of Rome and Carlotta was in Tracy's dressing room. She noticed a stunning frock on the wall and held it up to Tracy. "Where did you get this—are you wearing it for this commercial?"

"I thought I would," Tracy said, "the clothes they gave us were so lousy—and since this is a soft-drink commercial, well I thought I'd wear one of my own designs."

"Yours!" Carlotta was astonished.

"Yeah. I did that—oh—about six months ago."

"Smashing," Carlotta said. "Tracy, you never cease to amaze me."

A few minutes later, Tracy stepped out into the sunshine. She looked around the set and saw Sean perched on a high overhead camera crane.

"For Christ sakes, kid," he said, "you're holding up

the whole crew. We're ready to make the shot and you're not even dressed."

"I am too," Tracy said. "What do you call this?"

"Never mind what I call it," Sean snapped, "I'm talking about the stuff the client wants you to wear. Get with it."

"Oh, come on, Sean–for soda pop! I thought it wouldn't matter if I wore one of my own things. I can use the exposure."

"Exposure," Sean said, getting down off the crane. "Yes, I suppose you can."

"I mean, how else am I going to get my designs around," Tracy said. "This way, people will get to see a little of my stuff, and when I try to sell somebody, I can always say 'I've got film on this number' or that."

"I appreciate that, Tracy," Sean said. His face was tight. "But it happens to be wrong for the bit that we're doing."

"No it isn't, Sean," Tracy protested. "I've thought it over and I think it's exactly right, in fact. I want to wear it and I'm going to wear it. I told you, I want the exposure."

Sean turned away and glanced at Carlotta, who had moved close enough to take in this scene. Carlotta was careful to reveal nothing in her expression.

"OK, Tracy," Sean said, turning back to face her, and then, with one vicious swipe, tearing the whole front of the dress away from her body.

"There's your exposure. That do it for you?"

She swung–and connected. Right across his face.

Back in the dressing room, when Tracy had composed herself and was stretched out on the sofa with a cigarette, Carlotta knocked and entered.

"Tracy," she said, "I don't blame you if you refuse to work with him again. And I promise you, I can get other photographers who are just dying to use you. Believe me, you won't starve."

"I have no intention of starving, Carlotta," Tracy said. "And in fact, it's high time I started to get my designs before the public and I'm determined to do it."

"I can do a lot for you if you'll let me, Tracy," Carlotta said. There was something in her tone that caused Tracy to turn around and stare at the woman. And what she saw shocked but did not frighten her. Carlotta's face shone with desire and with something like love. Tracy shrugged. A few months ago this might have sent her howling out of the trailer. I guess I'm growing up, she thought. I can afford to live and let live.

"Carlotta," Tracy said. "All bullshit aside, will you tell me what you think of that dress?"

"It's good, I swear it," Carlotta said. "I know talent when I see it, Tracy and you've got it. But surely you must know that."

"Thanks, honey," Tracy said. "Working around that man, a girl sometimes forgets who she is. I think it's time that the public sees the real me."

Carlotta paused to nibble at one of her expensively manicured fingernails. "You know, Tracy," she said thoughtfully, "it occurs to me that there is a solution to your problem. I'm talking about Princess Galitzine's charity fashion auction, of course."

"Of course," Tracy echoed, "only I don't know what you're getting at."

"Well, to begin with," Carlotta said, "you are naturally going to volunteer your services as a model."

"I am?" Tracy said, amazed, and then, "like hell I am."

"No, dear," Carlotta said patiently, "I mean yes, dear, you are. Because I said you are. Because you're Gavina's top model and in fact, the most sought-after model in Europe. And when you occupy that position you have certain obligations. It's like being a member of the royal family."

"Well, forgive me, darling," Tracy said acidly, "but I sent my crown out to be cleaned and pressed and you know us royal types wouldn't be caught dead without a clean crown."

"I don't think you understand. This is probably the

most important social event of the season, to say nothing of its importance in the fashion world. Each year Princess Galitzine organizes this auction of fashion originals–not only her own, but from every major house in Florence and some houses in Paris and Madrid as well. I'm afraid it's a must, darling. No way out of it."

"OK, Carlotta, if you say so. I'm sorry if I'm showing my ignorance of tribal customs."

"Of course, darling, I don't blame you–you're a professional. But there's something else–" she hesitated.

"Go on," Tracy said.

"Well, you were talking about getting your designs to the public, no? And I was thinking–I mean, when you're alone in the dressing room you can put on whatever you want, no?"

"Yes."

"And when you come out when they announce you, and you're wearing something other than they'd planned for you, it's too late for them to do anything about it, no?"

Tracy was silent for a moment, frowning. And then suddenly her expression changed to conspiratorial delight. "Oh, Carlotta, you devil you!"

"And why not?" Carlotta shrugged. "You're offering your services absolutely free–for the sake of charity. We get no commission. Why shouldn't you offer *all* your services–your brain as well as your body?"

"Honey," Tracy said gratefully, "I couldn't agree with you more. You're dynamite!"

Carlotta shrugged. "It isn't possible for a woman to succeed in business in Italy if she's totally honest, *cara*."

"Don't worry," Tracy grinned, "I'd *never* accuse you of that."

A week later Tracy found herself nervously attended by Carlotta in a dressing room behind the grand ballroom at the Excelsior Hotel. The scene was something like a highly specialized zoo. Top models from all over Italy and France, even from as far away as London, sat around in various states of dress and undress waiting for the fashion auction to begin. Many of them were already wearing Princess Galitzine's latest originals, protecting necklines and armpits with wads of Kleenex. Some of them still had their hair in rollers, others were waiting for makeup women to apply body makeup to their bare breasts and thighs. Altogether, they looked like a gathering of graceful, overbred antelopes, eyes wide and vacant, lips twitching, moving with long, stalklike motions or draping their slender bodies on chairs and couches.

Princess Galitzine, a charming if imperious doyenne of Rome's haut monde, swept into the room. Not only was she the directress and inspiration for one of Europe's top fashion houses, she was also an acknowledged leader of beautiful people all over the world. She spotted Tracy instantly and came up to her, taking her hand.

"Ah, Mahogany," she said in her beautifully clipped English, "how very good of you to come to our party. You are kindness itself, my dear."

"As you know, principessa," Carlotta said, "Mahogany's schedule is sheer madness–but she managed to save some time–"

"I wouldn't have missed it for the world, princess," Tracy said simply, "and besides, I owe you something. I was wearing your clothes when I got my start with Gavina."

"And the audience will adore you," Princess Galitzine said. "I cannot tell you some of the people who are out there. But believe me, if the roof were to fall in, half the millionaires in Europe, the Near East, and South America would be wiped out. *À bientôt*, I must rush, darling."

"She's got a lot of style," Tracy said. "I like her. There's something very tough and strong under that glittering facade. You think I ought to go through with this, Carlotta?"

Carlotta shrugged. "What have you got to lose, darling? As Mussolini used to say, '*Meglio vivere un giorno come leone, che cento anni di schiavitù.*' Which means, 'Better to live one day as a lion than a hundred years as a slave.' "

"I can dig that," Tracy said. "You're talking to somebody who ain't got much use for the slave business."

Carlotta grinned and then said, "Come on, we've got to get you in that dressing room. I brought a small iron along with me in case the dress got crushed."

Out in front in the ballroom a handsome stage had been set up, banked with flowers, an orchestra on one side and of course, Rome's ubiquitous paparazzi (freelance photographers) popping flashbulbs throughout the crowd. The crowd itself was one of the most distinguished to be found in Europe. Not only were all the Italian aristocrats there, but many fashionable people from all over Europe and the civilized world were in Rome for the season. Some had come from Switzerland and as far away as Istanbul.

The house lights dimmed and the music faded to silence. An expectant hush fell over the assembly and for the moment there was almost no sound but the tinkle of champagne glasses and a few irrepressible murmurs.

"Ladies and gentlemen," the handsome announcer said as he stepped through the curtains to a spatter of polite applause. "So many of you have been here before that I will not tax you with a description of the proceedings. Do let me remind you again, however, that all of the profits that are earned here tonight are donated to the Foundation for Orphan Children which has been so close to Princess Galitzine's heart. Many of you are dear friends of hers and will of course, share her sympathy. And to those of you who have not been here before, I beg you, on behalf of the children, do be generous in your bidding. So, without further words–maestro"–he signaled to the bandleader–"the summer collection of Princess Galitzine is now on view!"

There was a cheerful round of applause. Spotlights shone on the curtain and a moment later a tall slender girl glided through the velvet drapes wearing a dazzling floor-length costume of finely jeweled chain. The effect was dazzling, as if she had burst forward with a cloud of ice crystals barely covering her beautiful nude body, undulating as she walked. The applause was loud and genuinely enthusiastic.

"The model is the famous Laura," the announcer said, "and she is wearing Borealis, I repeat, Borealis. May I hear the first bid? The first bid, please. Do I hear two million lire?"

A voice shouted out, "Two million, one hundred thousand."

"Oh, come, signori," the announcer chided, "you are not even warm yet. Do I have two-and-a-half. Bravo! Two-and-a-half. Do I hear three? Three, anyone. Three million lire? Two million, seven hundred fifty —very good, sir. Two million seven hundred fifty once, twice, and SOLD for two million seven hundred fifty thousand—to the gentleman on my right. One of the young ladies who are assisting us will approach you and take your pledge. And now," the announcer said, turning back to the proscenium, "we have the fabulous Danka—from Berlin, and she is wearing—"

And so it went. Another gorgeous girl wearing another one of Princess Galitzine's rich and imaginative costumes.

In one corner of the ballroom, quite apart from the stage, a very handsome and distinguished-looking man took up a position near a pillar and lit a thin cigar. Although his movements were quiet and totally without ostentation, it was not possible for him to escape notice. There was something powerfully magnetic about the man—and not just for women, but for men too. Heads inclined and there were whispers, "Il Gaucho, Don Cristiano Rosetti."

He was not unaware of these murmurs, had been

hearing them, in fact, all his life, but he pretended to take no notice. It was his custom to be solitary when he chose and he chose to do so now, neither acknowledging the direct stares of the curious nor the discreet hand waves of people he knew.

Carlotta Gavina, however, who was as brazen as she was beautiful, was not deterred by his passion for anonymity. Besides they had long been, and in several different ways, friends. "*Ciao*, Cristiano," she murmured, touching his arm in the darkness and indicating her unlighted cigarette.

He whispered a silent greeting and lighted her cigarette for her, allowing his hand to touch hers in a way that suggested old memories for both of them. "There was a rumor that you might be in Rome," Carlotta said, "but then there are always rumors about your movements. You're looking handsome as always."

"*Grazie, cara,*" he whispered, "the absence of light is beginning to suit me very well."

"Nonsense," she said, "you're the handsomest man in this room and always will be. What brings you to Rome?"

"What I like about you so much is your naked curiosity, my dear. Nothing will prevent you from asking the most tactless question if it suits your purpose."

"And nothing will prevent you from avoiding the answer with the most questionable compliment," Carlotta said, smiling slyly.

He chuckled. "I'm here to do business with Agnelli. Surely you must already have known that. You know everything."

"*Da vero!*" Carlotta was genuinely surprised. "You're going to buy him up?"

"Something like that," he said, "but I'd prefer it weren't talked about yet. Count Agnelli," he said, laughing softly, "doesn't know about it yet and isn't going to enjoy it when he finds out."

"Only in South America," Carlotta marveled, "could there be so much money."

"I can rely on you, my dear? I always could in the past."

"You know better than to ask that," Carlotta said quickly. "Oh, and by the way, when all of this nonsense is over, there is someone I want you to meet."

"A new girl?" his eyebrows rose.

"Like no other," she said simply.

"I believe that," he said, kissing her hand briefly. "How could there ever be another girl like you?"

Meanwhile the auction continued, building to the expected climax. "And now, ladies and gentlemen," the announcer intoned, "we come to the high point—the model all Europe is waiting for, the inimitable Mahogany"—he was interrupted by a round of applause. Holding up a hand, he continued, "wearing Princess Galitzine's most classic, most timeless model of white silk jersey and entitled 'Moonstone'!"

There was a chorus of murmurs from the crowd and a ripple of excitement. The curtains parted, the spotlights came on, and Tracy stepped out onto the runway in the center of the stage. She paused and then began a slow, sinuous stride.

There was an immediate hum of polite voices and this hum grew louder and louder as excitement rose. Tracy was not wearing a white silk jersey of classic simplicity, she wasn't wearing one of Princess Galitzine's gowns at all. Instead, she was strikingly—and shockingly—draped in a skintight ocher satin gown which fitted her lithe form like the skin of an exotic serpent. And on the bodice and skirt of this gown was a bright azure dragon in the Chinese fashion, coiling about her breast and hips.

Carlotta, standing alone in darkness, swallowed silently and muttered a Hail Mary to herself.

Not far away the Princess Galitzine let her champagne glass fall with a dull tinkle on the carpet. She could scarcely believe her eyes.

The announcer, trained in quick recovery, checked his program briefly and then smiled nervously at the crowd. "There, uh—has been a substitution, ladies and gentlemen—may I ask for the first bid. The first bid, if you please—ah, yes, you sir?"

It was Sean McAvoy, weaving slightly from too much champagne, who rose from his chair. "I bid five hundred," he said, his voice thick with wine and malice.

"Thank you, signor," the announcer said. "I have a bid of five hundred thousand lire, do I hear–"

"I said five hundred *lire*," Sean said loudly, "*not* five hundred thousand!"

This brought a nervous laugh from the crowd.

"*Va bene*," another man shouted, "one thousand!"

"I'll make it twelve hundred," said still another bidder. And by now, the tide of amusement was running strong. It was Rome, after all, the same Rome where people had at one time watched Christians being thrown to the lions–and their tolerance for blood sport ran high.

"Ladies and gentlemen," the announcer said, desperately trying to restrain the savage joy that was threatening to overtake these most civilized people and turn them into a bloodthirsty rabble, "this is no time for joking–don't forget the object of our auction, the Foundation for Orphan Children. So, now, may I hear serious bidding?"

"Sure," Sean called out. "I don't mind going higher in a good cause. I'll bounce it to fifteen hundred lire."

For Tracy standing quietly out there in the center of the stage, it was the undisguised viciousness in Sean's voice that finally undid her. What, she thought, have I ever done to make him want to hurt me so much. Her body trembled and she was close to tears. She was desperately fighting to regain her composure while every instinct prompted her to cut and run.

"I say twenty million lire," a strong voice called out.

"I beg pardon–" the announcer said, not certain that he'd heard correctly. This whole evening was beginning to fall apart for him.

"You heard me correctly," the voice repeated. "Twenty million lire. Over here." It was Cristiano Rosetti who spoke.

"Yes, of course, signor," the announcer said hastily,

"do I hear more? No? *Allora*, twenty million lire once, twice, twenty million lire–and sold! To the gentleman–"

Someone whispered the name to the announcer, but he did not repeat it. Gesturing wildly to the orchestra and to the stagehands, he led the crowd in a round of applause as Tracy gratefully retreated from the stage.

A short time later, Tracy carried the gown, beautifully wrapped, to its new owner. It was the custom after the show for Princess Galitzine to introduce each of the models to the generous benefactors who had bought the dresses. It was considered an obligation for the gentleman in question to invite the model to dinner and equally obligatory for her to accept. In this way, in fact, some of the most brilliant–and costly –friendships in Europe had been formed.

In Tracy's case, however, the Princess Galitzine did not make the introductions. In fact, she managed to ignore Tracy totally after the show. It was Carlotta who brought her to the man called the Gaucho.

"Cristiano Rosetti," Carlotta said simply, "this is Mahogany."

"*Enchanté*," he murmured, taking Tracy's hand.

"I don't know what to say," Tracy said honestly, very close to tears.

"Then please," he said, smiling warmly, "do not try to say it. And since you have lost your power of speech, then surely you will not refuse me the pleasure of having a drink with you."

Tracy managed a laugh. "Mister–at these prices, I think you're entitled to just about anything you want."

"How generous of you," he said, laughing, "but a drink will do me just fine, thank you."

And as he escorted her to the bar, bowing to friends on the way, occasionally throwing a kiss to a lady, Tracy's spirits began to rise. He was surely one of the handsomest men she had ever seen–not young, old enough, in fact, to be her father, but with a kind of strength in his expression and vigor in his movement that gave her a sensual thrill. As they moved into the crowded bar and as the crowd parted deferentially ahead of them, she noticed Sean smiling ironically at her from a distance. He raised his glass and she quickly turned her head away.

"You were absolutely marvelous in that dress," Cristiano said.

"Is that why you bought it?" Tracy said.

"Of course. I buy only what I like."

"Carlotta told me," Tracy said, "that although they call you the Gaucho, you own half of Argentina."

"Not quite half," he laughed. "That's a rumor started by my enemies."

"Oh? Do you have many enemies?"

"Quite a few, in fact," Christiano said slyly, "all those who own the *other* half of Argentina."

Tracy laughed delightedly. She began to feel comfortable in his presence and had forgotten her disgrace.

"Now, you must tell me," he said, "how did you happen to make that dress?"

"Who told you that?" Tracy asked quickly, "did Carlotta–"

"No, no, no," he said patiently, "I assure you, it was not Carlotta. I'm not a fool, after all. You were not wearing the Princess Galitzine's dress, and from the way you did wear that dress it was plain to me that it was your own creation. Am I wrong?"

"You're absolutely right," Tracy said, marveling at his insight.

"So. It isn't enough to simply be beautiful and be one of the most sought-after women in Europe," he said teasingly, "you want to prove that you have brains and talent as well, eh?"

"You flatter me too much," Tracy said. "I'm not really beautiful–that's a matter of current fashion. The trend. People see me *as* beautiful, I suppose."

"And people see me *as* rich," he said.

"Well, you were," Tracy said, "until you decided to go shopping for original creations."

Rosetti laughed and motioned to the bartender for another round of drinks. Relieved that this nightmare of an evening was turning out to be so pleasant after all, Tracy began to feel quite relaxed. Although she was hardly in the habit of flirting with older men, she found herself doing so, and enjoying it too. In fact, she was surprised to discover that, deep inside her, all the lights were turning green and she was additionally stimulated by a sensation that Cristiano was aware of that.

She was interrupted by a touch on her elbow. It was Sean McAvoy and he was atypically drunk. "Uh, Tracy," he mumbled, slurring his words badly, "I wanna talk to you."

She quivered with anger. The sound of his sardonic voice calling out "Five hundred lire" still echoed hotly in her mind. "We have nothing," she said acidly, "to talk about. Not now. Maybe, not ever."

"It'll only take five minutes," he persisted, not quite able to focus his eyes on her.

It was embarrassing. On the one hand she wanted to vent her anger, lash out at him. And on the other hand, she was confident that a terrible scene would ensue. "Sean," she said grimly, trying to suppress her fury, "I'm busy at the moment."

"No, no, no," Cristiano said generously, sensing her discomfort, "I was just leaving, Mahogany–business to attend to. We'll meet again, *chérie*, I'm sure of it." He kissed her hand briefly and left with a warm smile.

"Sure, he's sure of it," Sean said woodenly, "he can buy and sell us. He can buy this whole damn country if he wants. Look, Tracy–" he turned back to her, making a valiant effort to be sober. "Let me drive you home. I'm contrite, OK? I just want you to see me as you've never seen me before–humble, for Christ sakes!"

"I don't want to see you humble," Tracy said. "I don't need your apology. I don't want to see you, period. Do you read me!"

Sean blinked vacantly, digesting this information.

But he returned to his purpose. "Yeah, well—there's this party, you know, and you're the guest of honor. Somebody's got to escort you. You can't just walk in by yourself."

"Yes I can," Tracy said grimly, "and I will. The one thing I don't want is to see any more of you tonight." And with that, she turned on her heel and left him.

Seven

The following morning Tracy lay in bed chatting on the telephone with Carlotta, doing the usual girl-talk postmortem of the party the night before. Actually, the party had been fun for Tracy, even more fun than if she had been escorted by Sean. Best of all, Princess Galitzine, showing herself to be a true aristocrat, showed not the slightest trace of ill will and, in fact, complimented Tracy on the startling originality of the gown she'd worn.

"Of course you must understand, my dear," the princess had said, "that one design does not a collection make. Any more than one poem makes a poet. Still, I have been in this field long enough to know talent when I see it, even for a moment, it is unmistakable. And you have it, my dear."

"Then you're not furious with me for—well, for using you in this way?" Tracy had said.

"Certainly not!" The princess had laughed. "An artist must be ruthless, Tracy—utterly without conscience, except for fidelity to one's art. There one must never, never compromise. But using people?—my dear girl, if I dared to tell you the things I have done to make my way in the world, it would shock you into insensibility."

And so the incident was closed and Tracy was able to enjoy her role as the newfound darling of Roman society. Her "little prank" as it was called, her "caprice," gave her additional stature. She was not only exotically beautiful, she was also a daring young woman.

Now, on the telephone with Carlotta, she recapitulated the highlights of the previous evening. "You mean we really made the gossip columns!" Tracy marveled.

"But all the time I spent with him was—let's see, we had one drink after the auction, and then when he came by the party, I think I danced with him once. And by the way, he is some kind of dancer! It's that Latin blood, I guess, you know, they're naturals, like we're such good athletes!" She laughed at her own joke.

Carlotta joined her and added, "When the man happens to be Cristiano Rosetti, darling, anything he does is food for the gossip columns. Another thing—he doesn't just dance with anybody. I know it for a fact, even though he's good at it, he abhors dancing. So you must have scored quite a few points."

"Oh, well," Tracy said, "I don't suppose I'll ever see the man again, and if I do—"

She broke off, startled by an unusual sound just outside her door. It sounded as if someone had dropped a load of coins on the marble floor outside. "Uh, just a minute, Carlotta," Tracy said, "I want to check something out."

She got out of bed and tiptoed to the door and listened. Then there was another great splash of coins falling on the marble floor. She flung open the door with a whoop!

"It couldn't—" she said, "it isn't—I don't believe it!"

And then she soared up off the floor and into Brian Walker's arms. He held her against him in a bear hug for long seconds before they were both able to talk.

"What?" she breathed when he let her down, "what? —how?—when?"

"I just happened to be in the neighborhood." He grinned and indicated her brief, almost transparent nightgown. "Good thing I caught you dressed for company."

"Oh, Brian, thank God!" Tracy shrieked, hugging him and kissing him like a puppy maddened with delight. He lifted her up again with one arm, grabbed his suitcase, and carried her inside, closing the door with his foot. "Now," he said, putting his hands on her bare haunch and sliding up her body, "we've got some unfinished business to attend to."

It was a very long time before either one of them realized that the telephone was still off the hook, lying on the bed. Suddenly, Tracy spied the receiver, clapped a hand to her mouth, and then picked it up.

"Carlotta!" she muttered, "you—you're not still there?"

"Yes, darling," Carlotta said patiently, "and frankly, my dear, I'm exhausted. It's the first X-rated telephone call I've ever listened to."

Much later in the day, after they had recovered from the first torrid seizure of lovemaking and had passed into something like calm, Tracy padded in from the kitchen with a bottle of wine and a platter of sandwiches while Brian gazed appreciatively out of her windows. They had, without quite intending to do so, resumed an old argument.

"Brian," Tracy said almost wistfully, "I don't think you realize what it means for me to be a success. I am a success here. Naturally, I love the place. Love everything about it. Is that hard to understand?"

"No, of course it isn't, honey," he said, turning away from the window. "And looking out at that view I can't blame you at all. The point is, though, you *are* a success. You've got that settled now. So you can make it work for you, back in the States.

"You know how it is, Tracy, works that way all the time. Prophet without honor in his own country, all that jazz. Well, you go out, you make it big, and you come back. And people fall all over you. Hell, every magazine in the country has been running your pictures. That's what brought me over here. It drove me bananas. Here I was, trying to do my work, trying to put you out of my mind, and every time I turned a corner, there you were on a billboard or a newsstand, in a TV commercial. I finally decided, only way to get away from you was to come over here and drag you back." He laughed, but his eyes were serious.

"Oh, Brian, Brian," she murmured, leaning against him and rubbing her cheek against his arm. "Why is it we're always hassling each other? Why is it we can't live *with* each other and can't live *without* each other?"

"Is that the way it is with you, Tracy?"

"Yes," she said simply.

He looked into her eyes and nodded slowly. "That's the way it is with me too. I tried. God knows I tried. I've been out with half the chicks in Chicago—make that one-third, OK?—and nothing. I mean nothing. Looks like we got ourselves quite a little problem."

"Couldn't we," she said, "just sort of enjoy ourselves for a while? I mean, look out there—Rome! Look at those magnificent ruins, and they're all mine. They come with the rent."

"Yeah, I know," he smiled. "Back home, they call these ruins slums. Not ruins. And that's what we get with the rent."

"It's true," Tracy said. "In Chicago, if it's old they tear it down. It tears people up too, tears up their memories, their families. My God! I forgot. I've been rattling on—how'd it go? The election, I mean."

"Oh, that," Brian laughed. "Well, it's a long story—I lost."

"Oh, Brian—" Tracy's voice was filled with anguish.

"Hey, forget it," he said cheerfully. "That's history, all behind me. It didn't bother me any. I just blew my brains out two or three times and started hustling again. Seriously, I learned a lot. And most important, I've built up an organization. Next time I'm going to shoot for something much higher than alderman—and I'll make it, Tracy. I'm sure of that. There's only one thing—"

"What's that?"

"It won't really matter," Brian said, "unless you're there. You're part of it—in my mind."

Tracy didn't answer him. There was nothing that she could say. Instead, she kissed him, trying somehow to express her complexities of feelings that even she could not quite understand. The kissing helped, however. It was a kind of reality that couldn't and wouldn't be changed. So long as that feeling continued to exist between them, there had to be—there just had to be a way.

On the following day Tracy took Brian to her favorite trattoria, the place where she had her own table, her own napkin, where she was fussed over as she had never been at home. Brian couldn't help responding to the warmth of the place. And he was also reminded that in the last twenty-four hours they had scarcely taken the time out to eat.

As a genial old waiter came up to the table, Tracy tried to show off her mastery of the Italian language. "Oh, *cameriere*, *buon giorno*, *questo mio amico*, *de America—uh*, *nome*, *uh*, *Brian*, *molto politico!*"

"*Ah*, *buon giorno*," the waiter said, "*molto lieto a fare la conoscienza*, *e che cosa prendete oggi*, *signori?*"

"Uh, *che cosa?*" Tracy said blankly, "oh, yeah, *sì*, uh, *un po' di vino bianco*, *per favore*, and uh—menu?"

"Tracy," the waiter said kindly, "leave it to me, eh? I gonna give you something good."

"Uh, *sì*, *grazie!*" Tracy said.

"I take care of it," the waiter said, "you talk English to you young man. I fix."

Left to themselves, Tracy and Brian burst into giggles. "You're really heavy with that Italiano jive, baby," Brian said. "I mean, molto heavy-o!"

Tracy was not content merely to pick up the tab for a magnificent luncheon. Instead, she marched Brian up the Via Babuino into the Piazza di Spagna and after he had dutifully marveled at this colorful scene, led him triumphantly into Brioni, one of Rome's smartest shops.

"Hey, baby," he protested, "I don't need any clothes. My suitcase can't close now. And besides, my budget won't cover bread for threads."

"Never mind that, you male chauvinist pig," she said. "Now that you're in Rome, you gotta do as the Romans do. Be kept, that is. All the handsome young Italian dudes have some woman who's keeping them. I'm your woman, aren't I?"

"You are unless my tired old body is deceiving me," Brian said.

"OK, then I'm going to turn you into an instant Roman. I mean, you look good for Chicago, lover, but you lack that continental look."

"Jesus!" Brian said, fingering the price tag on a handsome suede sports jacket, "for that kind of money you could buy a Continental all right, plus a Cadillac thrown in. Come on, this is nice, but let's split, this joke is going too far."

"No way!" Tracy said severely. "Where do you get this notion you can't accept things from me? Doesn't your male ego permit you to be on the receiving end? Have you got some kind of macho hang-up?"

"OK, OK, you win," Brian said, slipping his arms into the jacket she was holding up. In a few moments the salesclerk came over, smiling and bowing, greeting Tracy with an exuberant "*Ah, Signorina Mahogany, che onore!*"

And within minutes, Brian was newly outfitted from head to toe in the latest fashion. It was bad enough having Tracy pay for all of this stuff, but when she began to argue and dicker with the salesclerk about the prices his urge was to flee from the shop. In the end the salesclerk allowed that, since it was for Signorina Mahogany and since she would be accompanied all over town by the handsome Americano, they would let her have a substantial reduction "for advertising purposes."

Once they were out on the street, Brian muttered, "Did you have to go through that number in there? I mean people don't do that kind of thing."

She gave him a long significant look.

"Do they?" he asked.

"Of course, Brian—this is Rome. No Roman with any self-respect would pay the prices they ask. Bargaining is what they expect."

"But I thought that was an old myth—something that American tourists do," Brian protested.

"I'm no tourist," Tracy said. "And now that you're all dressed up, neither are you. Besides," she added, "I had a purpose behind all of this. I mean in addition to wanting my old man to look the beautiful dude he really is. We're going to a party at Sean's tonight and I wanted you to look like you've been here all your life."

"A party! Hey, I just got here. Couldn't we just spend tonight alone—and maybe tomorrow night—"

"Brian, I live here, remember? The party's tonight. It'll be the hippest crowd in Rome. Partly I want to show you off, but also, I more or less have to attend—for business reasons."

"What kinda business you in, baby?" Brian said narrowly. "I mean, when you have to go to parties to make contacts."

"Well," Tracy answered casually, "they don't call me *la felice putana* for nothing, you know."

"La who-chy what-chy? What was that you said?"

"*La felice putana*—that's Italian for the happy hooker."

"I guess I asked for that," he said. "Now I'm gonna

lay it down for you. One more joke like that, one more bad, bad joke, and I'm going to turn you over my knee and show you a little male chauvinism where you sit, you hear?"

"Oh, I hope so," Tracy said joyfully. "Come on, let's run home. I'll think of something outrageous before we get there."

It was well after eleven when Tracy and Brian pulled up in front of Sean's house. Even this normally quiet residential street seemed to throb with music and a kind of electric energy pouring out of the tall floor-to-ceiling windows over their heads. Three local policemen, who had been handsomely tipped by Sean, patrolled the sidewalk, checking on the guests. They recognized Tracy immediately and bowed them inside.

Once upstairs they opened the door and let themselves into pandemonium—a very special perfumed, brightly lighted, and expensive pandemonium. Even Tracy, accustomed more or less to these goings-on, stood still for some moments and blinked. The scene which came to them in dazzling fragments through flashes of white-hot strobe light looked like a Fellini parody of something out of an old Jean Cocteau movie. At least half the hundred or more people in these rooms were outrageously dressed homosexuals, wearing everything from nothing to wild animal skins to Paris originals—complete with full makeup and hair styles. Some of them were gorgeous. One of these women came up to Brian almost immediately and began to remove her skintight sheath, exposing beautifully formed breasts, writhing provocatively before him, her tongue darting in and out of her exquisite mouth.

"Listen, Giorgio," Tracy said, "you put your dress back on and put your tits away before I tell your plastic surgeon on you and he won't do that transsexual on you?

"I mean some of these faggots really get out of hand," she said to Brian.

"You mean that–that–woman–I mean, you know, those dynamite boobs and all–"

"Oh, hell, that's just Giorgio. You can't *have* a party in this town without inviting him. He'll follow you around sobbing at you for days. Come on, let's meet some of these people."

In another moment, however, they were swallowed up by the crush. Someone fell on Tracy and whisked her away to dance, and Brian found himself being taken by the arm by two beautiful blondes, one of whom was surely a transvestite, but the other was so clearly and monumentally a Swedish Olympic swimmer that he felt that he was at least fifty percent on safe ground. "Ve haff a sister act," the Swedish girl said, "and you vill luff it. Yust come in the bedroom wis us and we blow your mind for you."

"Oh, Vera," the other "blonde" shrilled, "we can do a lot better than that. My God! you look really hung, darling," the "blonde" said to Brian, fumbling at his waistband. He slapped the hand away and found himself a drink.

He was just starting to sip his drink and sort out some of the jumbled impressions he was receiving when Sean McAvoy approached with Tracy on his arm.

"Good to see you again, Brian," Sean said pleasantly. "I'm especially grateful because you've restored the sunshine of her smile. Would you believe I can never get this girl to smile ever since she left Chicago."

"Bull," Brian said, "not according to the pictures I been seeing all over the place. She looked happy enough to me."

"Well, she's a good little actress," Sean said, "so tell me, what do you think of my place, my friends."

"They look like just plain folks to me," Brian said, laughing, "like the kinda people hang out in the rib joints and the unemployment lines."

It was Sean's turn to laugh. "Most of them have had the good sense to choose rich parents," he said, "and the rest–well, life is a hustle, you know."

"Oh, I can believe that," Brian said, "I've been hustled already and I barely got in the door."

"Brian's a do-gooder," Tracy said, allowing a small edge of irritation to enter her voice, "and do-gooders are prudish, you know."

"Well, don't knock it, Tracy," Sean said, "doing good is important. Just something that I never could get into, that's all. Now, my bag happens to be collecting. Inanimate objects," he said, glancing mischievously at Tracy. "I find objects are a lot easier to handle than people. They don't talk back."

"Well, I guess people are *my* bag," Brian said. "It's what makes me a politician."

"But politics move so slowly," Sean answered. "Myself, I believe in revolution. Quick change, violent change. It's healthiest in the long run."

"Only for the living," Brian said dryly.

"If you're not too much of a pacifist," Sean said, "I'd like to show you my collection upstairs. What do you say? I'm sure Tracy can get along without you for a few moments. I'd really like to get your impressions."

Brian looked at Tracy questioningly. He wasn't at all sure that he knew what was going on.

"It's up to you," she said neutrally.

"Come on, Brian, Tracy's a big girl now, she can take care of herself. And I'm sure you can too, can't you?"

Brian took a keen look at Sean and saw that the man was fit and muscular, but very thin. He was like a coiled spring. But Brian had played semipro halfback for four years and had been in street fights ever since he was five years old. He reckoned he could handle himself.

"I'll see you around," he said to Tracy, and murmured as an elegantly dressed young man came up to her, "don't get lost, it's a long way back to Chicago."

Sean led Brian up a narrow stairway and into the upper level of this duplex apartment. As they passed one bedroom they caught a glimpse of an extraordinary scene inside, at least five and possibly more people engaged in a form of group sex that looked like a mound of spaghetti. Sean thoughtfully closed the bedroom door, muttering, "Some people have bad manners."

Entering his own bedroom he paused and switched on the lights, noting that only two people, both of them women, were in his bed—and were totally oblivious to him. He switched the lights off again, motioned to Brian to follow him, and led him through an archway into a small locked study. Once inside Brian could see that the entire room was fitted out like a private arsenal. In corners of the room there were automatic and semiautomatic rifles, assault guns, even a Russian bazooka. On the walls were gleaming pistols of every imaginable kind, some of them antique, some of them the latest military models. On the desk was an Israeli assault rifle with a full clip of ammunition beside it.

"Here," Sean said, tossing a live grenade to Brian. "Just don't pull that ring or you'll arm it. Well," he said, "what do you think?"

"What do I think?" Brian said. "I think it looks like World War III. This stuff must have cost you a fortune. What the hell do you do with it, man?"

Sean shrugged. "It relaxes me. I like to come up here when the pressure gets too heavy. Here everything is —well, decisive. Concrete. No questions of taste, opinion. Nothing soft about it. It's all hard and clean and cold."

"It's hard all right and cold—about clean, I don't know," Brian said. "Depends on who's doing what to whom."

"Have you ever been in a war," Sean asked.

"Not unless you can call Nam a war."

"Well, you look like a passionate man," Sean said. "Surely at one time or another in your life you must have said 'I love you' to someone."

"According to you, that's war?" Brian said.

"Yeah. In a way. In a way it is. People try to conquer each other, possess each other. Unconsciously they try to destroy each other. It's a kind of war. Not a very clean kind."

"What is this clean business?" Brian said sharply. "You sound like a guy who has so much dirty on his mind that he's always talking about clean."

"You know, you may be right," Sean said, picking up a large machine pistol. "I never thought of it that way before. Now you take this gun, for instance. It's a pretty straightforward kind of thing, right? I mean, you *know* what this stands for, no doubt about it, right?"

"I guess," Brian said, getting a bit uneasy. Sean was waving the gun to emphasize his words and every now and then the muzzle crossed an imaginary line of sight between him and Brian.

"Straightforward," Sean continued. "You know that this thing can blow your head off, can cut you in half. So there are no doubts, no confusion about what its purpose is."

"Hey, listen, if you don't mind," Brian said, pointing to the gun barrel.

"Oh, I'm sorry," Sean said, laughing. "I get sort of carried away. Where was I—oh, yes. You see my gods are a camera and a gun. Both are totally truthful. Would you agree with me so far?"

Brian couldn't take his eyes off the gun, which, he discovered, was coming closer and closer to pointing directly at him. "I'm getting a little tired of this game," he said, and then broke off.

Sean had leveled the pistol directly at his middle and activated the slide. His face was white and steely, his eyes like two black bolt-holes, entirely free of any expression.

"All I have to do," Sean said, as he raised the gun so that he could sight it directly at Brian's head, "is to squeeze this trigger very slowly. It's a military trigger, you understand, there's a lot of slack in it. But still, if a man is in combat—"

Brian lunged, reaching out a hand and grabbing the

gun barrel, shoving it steeply up. With his other hand he grabbed Sean's chest and heaved hard, knocking him over the desk. Brian's lunge carried him onto the desk and over, sliding on top of Sean.

Together they struggled silently, fiercely. Sean tried to bring the gun muzzle down to Brian's head and Brian kept trying to force the gun out of his hand. Both men were damp with sweat and desperation. Brian found that Sean was amazingly strong but in the end he was no match for Brian's superior weight and muscle. He managed to get the gun turned around, pressing it against Sean's temple. And then the trigger fell.

There was an empty, hollow click!

Brian sighed and sat back on his haunches, wiping sweat from his face. Sean lay there still on the floor. Once more he pulled the trigger and let it click harmlessly against his skull. Then he began to laugh silently and maliciously, pausing momentarily to point a finger at Brian derisively and break into laughter again.

"Asshole," Brian said finally with deep contempt. He got to his feet and tucked his shirt in. "You crazy little asshole!"

He left Sean still lying on the floor laughing silently to himself.

Downstairs, his chest still heaving with exertion and shock, he looked around the madness of the lower floor trying to catch a glimpse of Tracy. He found her at last, doing a mad dance with a man who was wearing full war paint and the costume of a Sioux warrior.

"Hey," he said, taking her arm roughly, "let's get out of here. Now!"

"Brian," she protested, "we just got here. Let's have some fun."

"I had all the fun I'm going to have," he said grimly.

Alerted by his tone, she took another look at him. "What happened?" she said, alarmed. "You two didn't get in some kind of a fight, did you?"

"I don't know if you could call what we had a fight

or not," he said grimly, "but if that little motherfucker ever so much as looks at me again, I'm going to bust his head for him."

"Sean! Was he being bitchy again?"

"Hey look, Tracy." Brian suddenly felt tired and very old. "I don't want to talk about it. I'm going back. You coming or are you staying?"

"But I told you, I've got to stay," she protested. "These are my people, my life—it's another world, Brian."

"It sure is, honey," he muttered. "And you're welcome to it."

He walked out the door, found a taxi, and made his way back to the apartment alone.

For a long time after Brian left Tracy was in a state of shock and conflict. The happiness she'd known in the last few days was shattered and there was no replacement for it. She felt empty. Even worse, she had a keen sense that the future would be empty too. How did it happen? How could she have ever let herself believe that she and Brian would make it together—really make it? They were poles apart, planets apart. Her world was here, glittering, exciting, frantic—a make-believe world perhaps, changeable, fragile, and full of tension. But it was *her* world and it was right here, all around her. And Brian's world was five thousand miles away—eight thousand? She wasn't sure and it didn't matter. It might just as well have been a distant planet.

But because it was her world and she was a part of it and because it was impossible to stand still in that world, she soon found herself swept back into its center. Someone handed her a drink, someone else embraced her and left a joint in her hand. She found herself beginning to move to the beat of the music and soon she was dancing, throbbing, alive with excitement. Inside her there were voices clamoring to be heard, but the music was loud and she turned her mind away from the voices. She went with the music, giving it her soul and her body, slipping off her gown so that her skin was bare to the music and she could feel the beat on her naked flesh.

It was, she realized, as someone lifted her up on his shoulder, a kind of forgetfulness. And she let herself be carried, taken somewhere, by someone. It didn't matter whom.

Eight

At eleven thirty the next morning Tracy opened her eyes and shut them again almost at once. She was grateful, dimly grateful, that the bedroom was her own. She never knew when she got home or how. She had no recollection of where she had been or with whom. Her body was drugged with fatigue and alcohol and her brain was almost toxic with dope. Slowly, as feeling returned, she realized that she was wearing a nightgown—and had no recollection of taking off her clothes. Tentatively she touched her body and winced. There were sore spots, almost like burns, on her breasts and shoulders. Struggling to achieve recollection, she had a faint vision of having danced naked, holding a fat candle above her head so that hot liquid wax spilled on her gleaming skin. It was a hideous memory and she recoiled from it. Yet something nagged at her, something would not permit her to lapse into unconsciousness again. There was, she remembered, something odd, something atypical about her room. She opened her eyes again.

And then she saw Brian. He was sitting quietly in a straight chair near the door. He was fully dressed and his suitcase was at his feet, his raincoat folded neatly over his knees. That's what it was! Brian!—and now, all her memories rushed back with such sickening impact that she almost retched and groaned.

"I guess," he said dryly, "you're gonna make it after all. For a while there, you had me worried."

"What time is it?" she asked miserably.

"Getting on to twelve."

She was silent for a long time, knowing that she had to ask him a question and dreading having to ask it. For she already knew the answer.

"What—why are you—you know, sitting like that? Where are you going?"

"Home."

She didn't have to ask what he meant by that. Home was home. *His* home.

"I can walk over to the hotel," he said matter-of-factly, "and pick up the airport bus from there. Plane leaves at two o'clock."

Again she was silent for a long time. "I suppose," she said finally, "it hasn't been a very good trip for you."

"My trip's all right, Tracy," he said quietly. "It's your trip that doesn't seem too good for you." He paused and then added, "But I guess I can't change that."

Something stung her. She felt a bite of anger. "Change it! What makes you think I want it changed? Who gives you the right to change me, change my life? What did you even come here for if you want to *change* me? I like me the way I am!"

He shrugged. "Maybe the way you are isn't the way you were. I used to know a girl named Tracy Chambers, a girl—not a piece of wood. Tracy Chambers, not *Mahogany*. She was—well, tough and soft at the same time. I guess I miss that, the softness. It—I don't see it now."

"That's right!" she snapped, sitting up and glaring at him, not caring that her hair stood on end, her eyes were rimmed with red, her body showed welts beneath the thin tissue of her nightgown.

"The softness is gone! And you know why? Because I want to be a success, that's why. And I *am* a success. You can't *be* a success and also be a nice guy. You've got to choose. And I'll tell you something else, Mr. Big Man." Her voice rose, shrill with anger, and she leaned forward on her fists, blazing at him.

"You can't stand that! You can't stand *my* success. Because you want it so bad for yourself. And you're a *loser!* Even that wouldn't be so bad—but you begrudge it for me. Now—I've said it. And I'll be goddamned if I'll say I'm sorry."

Brian looked at her thoughtfully for a long time before he answered. He seemed to be pondering what she said. At last he spoke.

"You may be right," he said wryly. "Who knows? I'm no big winner, that's for sure. On the other hand —success? Your kind of success? I don't know as I want that, Tracy. What kind of success is it that leaves you all alone? Success is nothing without someone you love to share it with."

It was her turn to reflect. She paused briefly, but then refused to contemplate this new thought. Impatiently she got off the bed, went to her full-length mirror, and struck a pose, reassuring herself that her slender body was still vibrant, youthful. It would go on being that for a long time to come. Then she turned to face him.

"Bullshit, Brian!" she snapped. "I'm not alone. You saw all those people there. They don't just love me, they adore me. I've got the richest man in Rome, one of the richest men in the world, running after me. Alone? I could get on that phone right now and fill this room with people in half an hour. Brilliant people, talented, fascinating people."

He nodded. "I guess you could at that," he agreed. "And they'd all want a piece of you, a turn-on. You're a freak, Tracy, that's what they love. You're the nigger glamour girl. You're the kink of the week!"

"Damn you," she snarled, "damn, damn, damn you! That's the second time in my life you've called me a nigger. And it's the last time. Now do us both a favor and get the hell out of here. Don't walk, run! Split, will you? You come over here telling me how much you *need* me, you've got to have me. You need me because I'm a winner, baby. But you can't *have* me. And that's it!"

He stood up and picked up his suitcase. "*Ciao*," he said softly. "I'm pronouncing it right, right? *Ciao*. Oh, and that jacket"—he pointed to the suede jacket he'd left on the chair—"give it to someone more deserving. To someone who *adores* you."

He closed the door quietly as he left.

For the next few weeks Tracy lived as if there were two beings inside her slender body. One part of her, the innermost part of her, was wrapped in tightly coiled bandages of pain. It was as if she carried herself inside herself like a mummy—preserved, intact, but utterly hidden, removed from all contact with the outer world. And the other self was her public self, her professional self—sleek, glittering, bright, and vivid, always on the move, always on display.

She worked as if she had become addicted to work, hooked on it, needing it the way a junkie needs a fix. She took every assignment, turned nothing down, nagged Carlotta for more. Checks piled up on her dresser top like falling leaves and would have remained there if Sean hadn't come into her bedroom one day and discovered them and then deposited them to her account.

Even Sean was alarmed by her intensity—alarmed and worn by it. She worked from morning until late at night, taunting him, insulting him, scorning his weariness. Again and again she urged him to get on with it, light up another scene, break out a fresh carton of film. He had to take amphetamines in order to keep up with her and his own frail grip on sanity was beginning to slip.

They were insane, or becoming gradually insane, and neither one knew how to stop it.

One morning they were shooting a sequence in a brand-new $40,000 Maserati. Tracy was at the wheel and Sean was on a camera truck rolling a few yards ahead of her as she drove. The site was a partly completed superhighway still closed to traffic but offering a long paved stretch of gleaming bright concrete.

As she moved up to the rear of the truck for the nth time, Sean motioned her to slow down, but some impulse in Tracy caused her to ignore him. Deliberately she bumped the rear end of the truck.

Sean leaped off the truck instantly and examined the front end of the glistening red luxury car. One fender was slightly dented and there was a crack in the hand-rubbed enamel. He was furious.

"Is that a new kick?" he said. "You've got to fuck up a forty-thousand-dollar car? Do you know what that's going to cost me? I'm responsible for damages."

"Yeah, well," Tracy said dully, "you can afford it. I mean, you've earned a bundle on me, right?"

Sean's eyes narrowed with anger. "Are you referring to this commercial–or the whole thing? Our whole relationship?"

"Since when," Tracy said, "did this become a relationship?"

She stared at Sean, seeing that his cheek was starting to twitch. It was a danger signal, she knew that, but she didn't care anymore. Didn't care about anything. They were, she realized tiredly, both pretty far gone.

"Move over," Sean snapped.

"What?"

"I said *move over*," he repeated ominously. "I'm going to drive this car."

She slid over and he got in. He started the engine

and revved it up to a high-speed whine. "You look like hell this morning, you know that?" he said to her. "It's a good thing I've been shooting through the windshield and you're wearing sunglasses. You couldn't stand a close-up, you look like death."

She was about to reply but he let the clutch out and the car leaped forward, slamming her back against the seat.

"I know what you're doing," he said, seeming to have lost contact with her. It appeared he was talking to himself and she felt her stomach tighten with fear. "You're trying to destroy yourself," he said. "That's your business. But you're also trying to destroy me."

"Sean, you're crazy," Tracy protested, "and will you please slow down!"

She had to shout at him because the tachometer was going crazy as the needle climbed in low gear and the immensely powerful engine thrust them faster and faster down the highway.

"What did you say?" Sean shouted, a maniacal smile on his face now.

"I said, for Christ's sake, slow down!" she yelled.

He took his hands off the wheel and began snapping pictures of her as she stared at him in terror.

"Sean!" she shrieked.

"Great," he roared, "again! Profile. Again."

She lunged for the wheel but he knocked her hands away. The Maserati continued to pick up speed, seventy-five, eighty, eighty-five—

"Sean, stop it!" Tracy screamed at him, pleading.

"No! We're going on. You and me," he shouted. "Going on!"

"Sean—the road—my God!"

And then it seemed the world fell out of the sky. Slowly, slowly, turning ever so slowly. The world fell down and the sky was black. Sean had no face. His face was gone. She was tired and closed her eyes.

Three weeks later, Tracy's eyes opened in a room she had never seen before. There was a bandage around her head and the top of her chin, another bandage on her wrist, and a cast on one arm. Carlotta was sitting beside her. She looked at Carlotta for a long time before speaking. Indeed, she wasn't sure that she could speak and when she finally did, her voice sounded strange in her own ears.

"He's dead, isn't he? Sean?"

"It's what he wanted, darling," Carlotta said sadly.

Tracy thought for a long time. "No," she said, "he didn't really want it. He thought he could beat it. Had to try . . ." Her voice faded away.

"He almost killed you too, Tracy. But don't worry," Carlotta assured her. "You're going to be fine. There are no serious internal injuries and thank God, no horrible scars. You'll be on your feet again in a few weeks."

Tracy digested this information carefully. It seemed important, yet somehow it didn't feel important. There was something wrong, something missing, yet she couldn't quite think what it was.

"Where am I?" she said finally.

"In Cristiano's villa," Carlotta said.

"Cr–?"

"Rosetti. The man they call the Gaucho. You remember?"

"Yes–only–"

"He had you taken out of the hospital and brought you here. With the doctor's permission, of course. You've been nursed around the clock. There are three nurses on staff."

"Why?" Tracy asked. "Why?"

And then she caught another movement out of the corner of her eye. Cristiano Rosetti came into view. He was calm and handsome as ever, warmly commanding.

"I thought you could get better care here, Tracy," Cristiano said. "And the way you look proves it. You're recovering beautifully. By the way, Carlotta"—he turned—"have you arranged that meeting with the lawyers?"

"Yes, it's set for tomorrow at four in the afternoon. Everything's all arranged."

He nodded and turned back to Tracy. "You know," he said to Tracy, "when I was a little boy, I had to spend some time in a hospital—and it frightened me terribly. You're better off, we're all better off at home."

"But I have a home," Tracy protested weakly. "I have my own apartment."

"I took the liberty of moving everything here," Christiano said. "This is your own suite—totally private, and you can have your own servants if you like. For the time being, of course, you must obey the nurse. Doctor's orders."

Tracy looked around her at this splendid airy room; outside she caught a glimpse of magnificent gardens. The furnishings were elegant and simple even though the room had something of the air of a hospital room.

Carlotta rose and patted Tracy's hand. "I've got to run, darling, but I'll be back tomorrow. Now you mustn't worry about anything. You're going to be perfectly all right, I swear to you. And don't worry about working either. I've gone over your bank account and you're sufficiently rich so that you won't have to do anything for a year if you like. Now, get some rest."

"Thank you, Carlotta," Tracy murmured. Her gaze followed Carlotta as she went out the door and then Tracy turned back to look at Cristiano, who continued to sit where he was with the same calm and confident smile.

"You barely know me," she said to him, "and yet you've done all this. Why?"

He shrugged. "Perhaps I've nothing better to do. I'm sort of a meddler, a rich man's hobby. Let's just say that I feel someone has to look after pretty things."

"Me? A pretty thing?"

"No. You're a beautiful woman."

"But look at me! What on earth would you want with a cripple? God knows how long I'll be like this."

"Not long," Cristiano said, "you must believe me. Anyway, there's time to talk about that when you're fully recovered. And remember—you're under no obligation."

"Thank you," Tracy said simply. She sighed and closed her eyes. Then, as she lay there, two tears slipped down onto her cheek.

He took her hand and stroked it very gently. "Listen to me, Tracy," he said, "that's a very good sign, a very good sign, that you're able to cry. It means that your spirit is whole. As I knew it would be. But now you've got to stop crying. You must rest. Let your body tell you what to do—that and the doctors. Rest. Tomorrow I'm going to tell you what I've planned for your future. But for now, remember that you're completely safe here."

She believed him. His voice was warm, his touch was gentle. She never felt more protected in her life.

In the days that followed, Tracy felt her body healing and her mind healing, felt herself coming together again in a way that she hadn't believed possible. Sean's death was a source of grief which, she knew, would never entirely leave her. Oddly, no trace of her former anger remained. She could only pity him now, ponder the tragedy of this brilliant and talented man who, she now realized, was flawed with a terrible urge to destroy himself. That he almost destroyed her in the process was something she did not and could not despise. It was an accident, she reasoned, a matter of chance. The impulse was deep and uncontrollable; he had to kill himself—that she happened to be at his side when this impulse overtook him was not his "fault." Whether or not this was a valid surmise did not matter. Most important, this generosity of spirit enabled her to recover that much more quickly.

About Brian too she could be philosophical, although she knew she was to blame for his leaving her. She was more than a little crazy at the time he showed up in Rome, more than a little deluded about her so-called success, and decidedly more than a little insufferable. Bitch, she murmured to herself, as her mind went back over those brightly colored days. Nervy, crazy, arrogant little bitch. It was not pleasant or easy to confess these failings but it was necessary if she was to move forward. Brian was–everything, she admitted to herself. Everything that she ever wanted, would ever want again. And it simply wasn't possible. She wept, dried her tears, and consoled herself by knowing that in time this pain, like the pain of her broken bones and battered body, would belong to the past.

Each day Cristiano came to visit her in the morning and again in the evening. Sometimes he had to go out of town on business and then always he managed to call her just before she fell asleep. Always his smile was warm, confident, a kind of tonic, she realized. He delighted her with stories of people he encountered in Rome, never malicious or derogatory–he was too powerful, too self-assured for that. He contrived always to find something admirable, special about the people he dealt with.

"I've never met anyone like you before," Tracy said, "someone who has so little fear or envy. I used to think it was because you were so rich that you didn't have to put anybody down. But it can't be that. I've met rich people before and some of them are terrible."

"You flatter me, Tracy," Cristiano said truthfully. "I couldn't possibly be as noble as you make me out to be. On the other hand, it may help you to understand me if you know that my grandfather, and my father as well, were Italian peasants. My grandfather had nothing except his own two hands–an immigrant's hard hands. And my father too, up until he was fifty, had to work in his own fields from morning until night. He died a rich man but he never forgot where he came from. And the truth is that I have not forgotten either. It doesn't matter to me how much money I have because there is a small farm that I maintain in Argentina, just a few acres, and I know that even if I lost everything else, I could always go back there and make a living for myself, my family. Like my father and grandfather, with my own two hands."

He held up his strong, scarred hands for Tracy to see. And they were, for all of his elegance and magnificent tailoring, the hands of an Italian peasant.

One morning, as her recovery progressed, he took her in her wheelchair as he usually did, for a tour of the garden. This time, however, he made an abrupt turn at the end of one of the paths and took her in a direction they had never gone before.

"Where are we going?" she asked. "Every time I think I'm getting to know this gorgeous house, you show me something I haven't seen before."

"It's a surprise," he said quietly, "something I've been planning in my mind. You'll see."

"Cristiano, couldn't I get out and walk now? I'm sure I can walk if you let me lean on your arm."

"Of course you can walk, but not quite yet," he said. "When the doctor says you may get up, then you will. Now, don't worry. Be content with the fact that you have the highest-paid male nurse in all of Europe."

She laughed and then her laugh faded. They had come in sight of an old carriage house, which was the center of considerable activity. There were workmen going in and out of the place, painters, electricians, carpenters. There were trucks outside and cables coming through the doorway. And as Cristiano wheeled her through the door and into the center of all this confusion, Tracy could see that the place was being fitted out as a large design workroom. In the center of the room, in fact, was a large custom-made drawing table and desk piled high with all of Tracy's portfolios and sketchbooks. In another part of the room were a dozen sewing machines and worktables for seamstresses. Workmen were installing full-length mirrors in dressing rooms and the electricians were still wiring the overhead lights.

"Well," Cristiano said, "what do you think?"

"I—I'm afraid to ask," Tracy said. "Is it what I think it is?"

"You're looking at my latest business enterprise, a subsidiary of the Cristiano Rosetti holding company.

I think we will call this Tracy of Chicago, or perhaps Mahogany Creations. I leave the name up to you. The point is, you are looking at Rome's newest atelier of haute couture!"

Tracy was speechless.

He looked at her fondly. "I can't tell you," he said softly, "what your expression means to me. I have never felt so rewarded."

"I feel," Tracy said, reaching for his hand, "as if I've died and gone to heaven. You're giving me my future, Cristiano—my dream."

He kissed her gently. "I have a dream too. A dream of us."

"Oh, yes," she said, her eyes shining, taking his hand and pressing it to her cheek. "Can I say thank you?"

"You will thank me," he said sternly, "by obeying your doctor, getting well as quickly as possible, and getting down to work. This is costing me a fortune, after all, and I do not permit my investments to lie idle."

Tracy laughed. "What I like best about you is that I know you're not kidding. OK, partner, you're calling the shots."

A month later, a fully recovered Tracy—only an elegant ivory-knobbed cane lying on her desk showed that she still needed occasional relief—sat in the middle of her atelier. The scene was one of highly purposeful confusion. Almost a dozen women were bent over humming sewing machines. Another woman was pinning cloth on a form. There were two young girls in a corner painting sketches; repairmen and workmen were still moving about the premises, laying cables and hammering cabinets. Tracy herself was shouting to make herself heard over this racket, with a telephone in one hand and a glass of milk in the other.

"Don't give me that *non capisco* jazz, Armando," she shouted furiously. "You knew damn well we had to have these machines in good running order when we bought them, so you get someone over here right away to make them work. I said right away. *Pronto*, you *capisce?*" She slammed down the phone and grabbed another that was threatening to topple off the drawing board.

"I've got two days!" she shouted into the receiver. "Two days to get ready for that show. If you don't get that muslin over here by tomorrow morning first thing, I'm going to buy your damn mill and fire you. Is that clear!" Bang, went the phone.

Getting up quickly and without any trace of a limp, she went over to a sewing machine where a middle-aged woman was working with peau de soie.

"Damn it!" Tracy said with exasperation, "doesn't anybody understand me around here. You've got to have a double stitch or the hemline won't hold. Double! Do you understand?

"*Si, signorina*," the woman said, "*capisco, due fili, pero l'ago non e abbastanza fine*—"

"Shit!" Tracy snapped, throwing the fabric down on top of the seamstress's machine. "I haven't got enough trouble trying to put this all together, I gotta have language problems too."

"It's not a matter of language, Tracy," Cristiano said. He'd come in the door without her noticing him. He stood there with a faint look of disapproval on his face.

"It's a matter of tone," he said. "These people will understand anything if you use a different tone. You frighten them, don't you see?"

"Well, hell, I'm frightened too, Cristiano. I'm putting myself on the line and these clods aren't helping me."

"All very well," he said patiently, "but it's like working with hunting dogs, you know. If you betray your anxiety, you will make them nervous as well—then they don't perform well for you."

"I am *not* an animal trainer, for God's sake!" Tracy said angrily. "I'm a designer. And these are supposed to be the best needlewomen in Italy. I'm paying them enough to be topflight seamstresses."

"Uh, correction–*I'm paying* them."

"All right, I stand corrected. But I've gotta have these things by tomorrow so I can fit them on the models. It's your money but it's my reputation."

Cristiano sighed and murmured something soothing to the distressed seamstress, who had followed this conversation without appearing to understand it. She listened to him gratefully and smiled.

Tracy muttered angrily. "*Non capisco*, my ass!" she said scornfully. "It's just that she's a woman and I'm a woman and she wants to give me a hard time."

"Now that peace is restored," Cristiano said, "I'll leave you. Thank God my work is with engineers and oil geologists. I couldn't stand having to employ artists."

She gave him a quick, nervous smile and kissed his cheek. The telephones, all three of them, began to ring again.

Later that night, Tracy, wearing a long white robe, was stretched out on an enormous couch, staring up at the goddesses and cupids and chariots which adorned the palatial ceiling. She held a brandy glass in her hand and turned her head as Cristiano approached.

"Sorry I was unable to be with you at dinner, darling," he said pleasantly, "but I had a business emergency to deal with."

"I'm glad to know," she said a bit tartly, "that you have business emergencies too."

"A tanker with a hundred thousand tons of oil waiting to get docking space is a moderately serious problem," he said.

"I'm sorry, Cristiano," she said, her expression softening. "I realize my problems are piddling, but then they're all I've got. Forgive me for being such a little bitch."

"If I had to forgive you," he said, smiling, "I wouldn't be here. Oh–this is something that might amuse you." He handed her a small green velvet box.

Tracy opened it and saw a pair of magnificent diamond earrings in teardrop shape. "Oh, Cristiano!" she said, "they're gorgeous. But–"

"But?"

"Well–I mean, my God, I don't know that much about diamonds, we didn't see a whole helluva lot of them in the ghetto. But these would buy two or three oil tankers. Cristiano–" she hesitated.

"Yes," he said patiently, "go on."

"You've already done so much–"

"Business," he said, holding up a hand, "strictly business."

"I–it's hard to say this–but I don't want you to think you have to buy me."

He laughed. "It never occurred to me that it was possible. And if I thought I could, I shouldn't have tried." He paused. "Rather, it's the other way around. I should like you to own me, Tracy."

"Me!" she sat up, startled. "That's crazy. I'm–I'm nobody. I'm Tracy Chambers, that's all. A skinny little black chick from the Chicago ghetto, and you're–"

"Nonsense." He put a finger against her lips. "You are a slightly unstable and enormously talented young woman–who just happens to fascinate me," he said simply. "And after tomorrow night, despite all of your worries and your crises of temperament, you are going to be the most successful designer in Rome. I have no doubt that, by the end of the year, you will be the leading designer in all of Europe."

"You believe that, don't you," Tracy said, looking into his eyes.

"If I didn't believe that," he said, "I wouldn't have invested in you. I'm not in business for my healthy, you know."

She laughed. "Health, not healthy," she corrected him.

"Never mind," he smiled. "I want *you* to be healthy, and that means you must go to bed now. And I want you to be beautiful. For tomorrow night."

She kissed him meekly and went upstairs. As she took off her clothes and got ready for bed she found herself frowning, puzzling over a problem that just wouldn't be solved. He's handsome, she told herself, cultivated, warm, witty, intelligent, strong and rich. And he adores me. And he's the most sought-after man in Europe—perhaps the world. Which makes me the luckiest girl in the world. Then how come I don't feel lucky?

Just before turning off the light she stole a glance at the diamond earrings still in their little velvet box, reposing on her night table. Beautiful, she thought, just beautiful. But hard, and somehow cold.

Nine

The entrance to the Spoleto theater somewhat resembled the scene at a Hollywood premiere in the thirties. There were crowds of onlookers, cordons of police, with a special riot detachment stationed quietly and ominously in the side streets. Limousines drew up to the entrance, and under the bright lights of TV crews a steady stream of Europe's most distinguished theatergoers emerged from their cars and walked into the theater. It was, of course, a kind of theatrical event, a special showing, the maiden showing of Mahogany Fashions. The paparazzi, Rome's ever-present photographers, were going out of their hyped-up skulls.

Inside, the theater had been transformed into a kind of elegant cabaret. The entire floor of the orchestra had been emptied of its seats and in their place were small tables gleaming with glasses and bottles of champagne. Fortunately Cristiano owned, among his other enterprises, one of France's most ancient vineyards and he was able to provide these guests vintage champagne in quantities that might have bankrupted an ordinary man.

Cristiano was, however, no ordinary man. He had personally supervised the transformation of this handsome and venerable theater, banking it with flowers from his own estates, putting his own majordomo in charge of all the waiters and kitchen staff. He had also brought in his own staff of carpenters and artisans to execute the design motifs that Tracy had originated.

Backstage Tracy, quiet and tense, supervising last-minute touches and changes, was accompanied by Cristiano and Carlotta.

"It's almost time, darling," Cristiano said, consulting his watch.

"I know," Tracy said. "I just have to check out one or two more items. Why don't you and Carlotta go out front and I'll join you in a moment."

"I wouldn't dare leave you at a time like this," Carlotta said. "If it were me, I'd be hysterical by now."

"You don't understand," Cristiano said fondly, "when the pressure is at its greatest, this is when she is most calm. Come along, Carlotta. Tracy—" he kissed her. "As they say, break a leg."

A flicker of a grateful smile crossed her face and then she bent to remove a bit of thread from a model's skirt as she passed by.

As the houselights dimmed to black an expectant hush fell over the crowd. Suddenly a very narrow spot came on, illuminating an area no larger than a silver dollar on the black velvet curtain. Into this spot came Tracy, wearing a formfitting silver lamé sheath. She gleamed like a delicate blade.

The crowd broke into a tumult of enthusiastic applause. Whatever else might ensue, Tracy, as her own creation, was surely a success.

She waited patiently for the applause to fade, holding herself very straight and very still. Then, dramatically, she spread her arms and called out, "*Mesdames et messieurs*—I offer you the Mahogany line!"

There was another round of applause, the spotlight vanished, and Tracy withdrew. The orchestra struck up an oriental overture and suddenly, strange and beautiful forms began to appear on the black velvet curtain. The designs seemed to be made of light itself and took on an abstract oriental quality, swaying slightly, turning slowly, as if they were animated.

And then, as the crowd gasped with appreciation, the lights rose in intensity and they could see that these designs were, indeed, animated. They were light-sensitized garments worn by models standing on different elevations all over the backstage. The effect was both startling and magical, as if these light movements had been transformed into beautiful women and then, ultimately, into beautiful gowns.

One by one the models, moving with stately elegance and in time to the music, came down from their platforms, crossed the stage, and moved out onto the long runway which thrust like a promontory into the crowd. The clothes they wore were all inspired by the same oriental motifs so that it seemed as if the audience were seeing a form of Kabuki theater. The audience gasped with genuine delight and broke out frequently into spontaneous applause. This applause had its effect on the models as well, causing them to experience the rising excitement and throw themselves into their roles as if they were actresses. The entire spectacle was taking on a different quality from the usual static fashion show—it was becoming a smash hit!

And after the models descended and made their stately walk down the runway, they returned to center stage and grouped themselves in a large semicircle. Now, into the center of this semicircle, holding a Kabuki mask in front of her face, and wearing the most spectacular costume of all, came the last model. The others raised their arms in greeting.

Slowly she moved forward with a kind of ritual step as if she were a high priestess of fashion, and as the music swelled to a dazzling crescendo she slowly drew the mask away. The effect was stunning and totally dramatic. She was none other than Mahogany herself! The crowd, elegant, jaded, accustomed to sedate forms of approbation, went giddy and wild. There were shouts, whistles, bouquets hurtled through the air, and the audience rose spontaneously to their feet for a long and heartfelt ovation.

Tracy bowed deeply, extended her arms as if embracing these well-wishers and returning their affection. Then, unable to bear it any longer, turned and ran backstage.

She subsided gratefully in Cristiano's embrace and submitted as he blotted the tears that were welling out of her eyes. It was some time before she could trust herself to talk.

Carlotta was breathless with excitement. "Tracy, Tracy, Tracy," she squealed. "You've done it. There's never been anything like this. Never! I've been assured of half a dozen cover stories in the biggest magazines in Europe. The man from *Time* promises a feature story—maybe a cover there as well. Cables have been pouring in—bids. Look—" She thrust a sheaf of cables at Tracy.

"You're going to be so rich, darling," Carlotta raved on. "You're going to be the queen of fashion, the reigning queen!"

Tracy stared at Carlotta, her eyes still wet with tears, unable to comprehend all this gibberish. Sensing her confusion, Cristiano led her gently away through the crowd of models, newspaper people, stagehands, who were all milling around backstage.

"I know you want to go home," he said gently.

"Oh, yes, please," Tracy murmured gratefully.

"And you will, but I think you owe it to them—just one last bow. Go ahead, I'll be standing right behind you."

Numbly, scarcely able to let go of his hand, Tracy

went out in front of the curtain once more, felt, rather than heard, the beat of thunderous applause, threw the crowd a kiss, and then ran back to the ever-protective Cristiano.

She huddled in a fur robe in the back of his limousine, scarcely saying a word as they drove up the long mountain roads to his villa.

Once inside, when she was seated with her legs curled up beneath her on the couch, Tracy gratefully accepted a brandy from Cristiano.

"It's a little terrifying, isn't it," he said. "All that heat and energy that it took to create this success—and then when it finally happens, you're left empty and cold."

She nodded, unable to speak. She couldn't tell him what she was feeling because she could hardly understand it herself. But she was fighting down the impulse to flee. Flee where? Why? She didn't understand. It seemed so insane. She had all Rome at her feet and all she wanted to do was run.

He stared at her intently, saying nothing, waiting for her to meet his gaze. When she did not, he finally spoke and his voice had an unfamiliar edge—dry, flinty.

"You know, Tracy," he said, "I think it is time for our life to begin—together. Do you understand me?"

She looked at him then, having barely understood his words and yet knowing what it was he was saying. But what he was saying, she thought, was quite impossible.

"What I'm saying," he persisted, "is there is a time for everything. And the time for us has come. I want you to get up and come upstairs. With me. Together. It is time."

"Yes, Cristiano," she said dutifully. Her mind told her he was right. Her mind told her that she was grateful to him, that she loved him, respected him. And her mind also told her that it was impossible.

Moving like a wooden doll, she put down her glass and crossed in front of him, heading for the stairs.

Upstairs, she passed her own doorway and walked into his bedroom. She was standing in the center of the room when he joined her. She seemed unable to move of her own will. Gently he took her shoulders and guided her to his enormous bed. She sat and he bent and kissed her. She made no motion.

He removed his jacket and his tie and threw them onto a chair. Then he took her face in his hands and turned it so that he could look into her eyes. She looked at him but her expression was vacant and as he bent slowly to kiss her, he saw tears begin to form.

"What is it, Tracy?" he whispered.

She shook her head, unable to answer.

He caressed her shoulders, slipped her strap down, and kissed her bare breast. She continued to sit, unmoving, and he finally took his hand away.

"You're very strong, Tracy," he said. "Very strong. I think you really would go through with it, wouldn't you?"

She shrugged finally and said, "Why not?"

"Why not," he repeated with an ironic edge. "Why not. It's no good, Tracy." He sighed. "No. It's no good. I don't want that from you. Not from anyone and especially not from you." His face was grave.

Suddenly she burst into tears. Her sobs were deep and racking. It was as if all the tension of the last few weeks, all the months and years of pain before that, had finally broken through her defenses.

He held her tightly until her sobs abated. When she was finally able to speak she said softly, "Cristiano, when you said 'I know you want to go home,' you know what I thought?"

"No."

"I thought you meant–go home to Chicago. It's what I want, Cristiano. What I want more than anything in the world."

He was silent for a long time. "You'd give all of this up?" he said gently.

"It was never mine. It isn't me."

He got up and paced up and down the room a few times.

"Are you angry? I don't blame you. I'd give anything if I–"

He silenced her with a wave of his hand. "Don't talk nonsense to an old man, Tracy. No," he frowned, appearing to be going over details in his mind. "We'll get you on a plane first thing in the morning. If no flight is available, I'll give you my own plane. Oh, and Tracy, I'm not going to shut things down immediately. I'm going to give you a month to think things over."

"But I–"

"No, you listen to me," he persisted. "We owe each other that–as a business proposition. I'm not talking about a life together. I realize now that will never happen. I'm talking about business. If in one month's time you still want to stay in Chicago, I'll dismantle the enterprise. Don't worry, in my tax position, it won't cost me much. Look at all the fun I've had–" He laughed.

Tracy went up to him and rested her head against his chest. "Cristiano," she murmured, "there never was anyone like you. There never will be again."

"Yes, I know," he said coldly, distantly. "Now you will please get out of this bedroom at once. Before I forget myself–and take the revenge I want!"

On the South Side of Chicago a large crowd was gathered around a red-white-and-blue van that was hung with bunting and posters proclaiming BRIAN WALKER FOR CONGRESS. It was a good-natured crowd and getting larger all the time as Brian Walker, back on his turf, bullhorn in hand, was going into his pitch.

"The polls say we're behind," he said. "Well, I got news for you. We *been* behind, we been behind in this country for better than two hundred years, but we ain't behind no more. We're goin' *forward.* You and I, together!"

This brought a roar of approval. Wil and some of Brian's other assistants grinned at each other. The man was going great. They were eating it up and the scent of victory was in the air.

A voice came out of the crowd. "Hey, what you goin' to do about high prices?"

"Pay 'em!" Brian shouted back quickly, "same as you. But in addition to that, I'm going to use *your* support and the support of all you other people out there to *do* something about it. Not talk. *Do!*"

"That's big talk," another voice called out. A woman's voice this time. "But I'm a widow from the South Side."

"Who said that?" Brian bellowed through his bullhorn, staring at the crowd.

"My old man left me with six kids," the woman continued, "the heat's been turned off a week, and the kids has all got the flu. Now what are you gonna do about that!"

And then Brian spotted Tracy as she edged out from behind some people in the crowd. He broke into an enormous grin.

"Madam," he said, "I may be able to help you with your landlord, if that's what you want."

"Hell no," Tracy laughed, "I want you to get my old man back." The crowd roared with laughter, enjoying the byplay between these two attractive young people, sensing the current that ran between them.

"I might get your old man back too," Brian shouted, "but I got to know if you're willing to stand by him if the going gets tough."

"Lord, yes! I'll stand by," Tracy shouted.

"Well, madam, if you'll just come right up here to the microphone and tell me you'll take your old man back for the rest of your natural life—"

He never did finish that statement. Tracy ran to him and leaped into his outstretched arms, while the crowd roared and stamped their approval.

"Oh," she murmured, kissing him feverishly, "it feels good to be home!"

He held her apart from him and looked into her eyes. "Only if you're willing to stay, Tracy–I can't get cut up like that again. You willing to make this your home?"

"You *are* my home," she breathed. "Wherever you are is wherever I am."

"Hey, Wil!" Brian called out. "You know what day this is?"

"No, man," Wil called back, delighted to see Tracy and the boss together again.

"This is the first day of the rest of our lives!"

I'm alive, Tracy thought. I'm Tracy Chambers and I'm alive. Who was Mahogany? What was Mahogany? Nothing, she thought. Just an old piece of wood.

ABOUT THE AUTHOR

BURTON WOHL was born in New York City and attended Hofstra University. For quite a few years, before turning to novel writing exclusively, Mr. Wohl worked as a journalist both in the United States and abroad, for *The New York Times*, *Time-Life*, Inc. and other publications. His previous books include: *A Cold Wind in August*, *The Jet Set*, *High Encounter* and three novels based on screenplays, *Posse*, *That Certain Summer* and *Mahogany*. Mr. Wohl is an avid backpacker who backpacks whenever he can find the time. He also raises Bonsai (Japanese dwarf trees) and has a pet long-haired dachshund, Grover. Burton Wohl presently lives with his wife and three children in Beverly Hills, California. He is at work on a new novel.

COFFEE, TEA OR ME? *by* TRUDY BAKER & RACHEL JONES

Here's the real lowdown on the high-flying stewardess scene jet-propelled your way by two audaciously outspoken young ladies who lived it and loved it.

There's the captain who makes like a 707 when he's wooing; the passenger who mistook the overhead luggage rack for an upper berth; the celebrities who are a pleasure to serve (with some surprising notables on the 'bad guy' list). Here is a gold-mine of anecdotes and outrageous information on the aerial and amorous adventures of the swinging young 'stews'.

"The kind of book that is a nuisance to own. Everyone wants to borrow it."—LOOK

0 552 8786 6—**50p**

THE QUEEN *by* MORTON COOPER

During the days before Judith Harrison's trial, Hartley filled with reporters from all over the globe, with her masses of supporters and armies of enemies, and with weird members of outlandish minority groups. When the trial began, it seemed that the eyes of the world were fixed on the little town . . . and on the proud, furious figure of Judith, defending her rights and freedom in a battle that was to make history. . . .

Powerful, sexy Judith swept through the male-dominated society she lived in like a cleansing wind which was building to hurricane force. Her story boldly explores the world of modern woman, her confusions and passions, her rages and triumphs. . . .

0 552 10011 0—**65p**